Agents
Risky Liaison

Ele Shev

PARTRIDGE
A Penguin Company

Printed in India.

Partridge books may be ordered through booksellers or by contacting:

Partridge India
Penguin Books India Pvt.Ltd
11, Community Centre, Panchsheel Park, New Delhi 110017
India
www.partridgepublishing.com
Phone: 000.800.10062.62

CONTENTS

INTRODUCTION

THE HOPE FOR ESCAPE

The night was young. The moon showed the silhouette of the girl, climbing the mountain. The grace of her stunning body was extraordinary. It seemed like she was floating in the cold air. The moonlight fell on the face of the girl. Her eyes were extremely beautiful. Even the strongest man would go weak in the knees just looking into her eyes.

But right now, you could see great tension in those eyes. She knew any step further could mean death. The girl stopped. She could feel that the first border is somewhere close. She was looking for a clue. Here it was: one rock looked larger than others as if taken from somewhere else. Its color was different as well. She took a small stone, lying near her feet, and threw it. "Mike was right," she whispered to herself, "You can't escape!" The invisible laser beams were right here. The stone was destroyed completely. It could have been her. One more step and she would have been dead . . .

The girl looked at her watch. She only had six minutes to make it back to the castle without raising the alarm. She had to hurry. Even professional climber would not dare to do this without any safety equipment. She had no choice. One last step and she jumped into the campus yard of gloomy castle.

Well, today she failed: she realized it could be next to impossible to escape. The girl moved the camera aside, counted thirty seconds, then moved it back and went straight to her room. She needed to get good rest before tomorrow's classes.

The next morning Angela woke up fresh, without feeling of defeat. She had once again in her heart hope for escape. One day, she'll find a way to get her freedom. She heard students laughing and joking. Everybody seemed to be getting ready for breakfast.

CHAPTER 1

MONACO

Angela entered the canteen and went straight to juice counter. Mike was there. She took a glass of orange juice and moved into a blind spot. Mike moved towards her. Angela looked at her watch: they had 90 seconds before the camera turned back.

"Mike, I tried to escape last night. You are right. It's impossible to cross the first border. I hardly made it back on time."

"Angela, I told you to be careful. You will get yourself killed for nothing. Anyway, I will send you new codes tonight. The password is Elias gamma + Fibonacci encoding. The number encoded is the day of the week in both cases."

"OK, cool, send it to me. Mike, also it is very strange. Deepika and Max just disappeared from the castle. I suspect something is wrong . . ."

"You're right, Angela," Mike interrupted, "something fishy is going on here. I'll try to hack their files. Sorry, I've gotta go now. Bye, doll."

"Bye, Mike." Angela looked at her watch again–only ten minutes left until class starts. She took her glass and went to food corner. She had salad and porridge. The food was delicious.

The assistant came to Angela and asked her to go to the professor's room. Angela's heart skipped a beat as she walked down the long corridor. "Did they find out about Mike and me?" she wondered. She entered the professor's room.

Mr. Wells told her, "Congratulations, Angela, you are selected for the mission. Go and pack your bags fast. You will leave in an hour."

"Yes, Sir!" she answered.

"Great," Angela thought, walking back to her room, "They didn't catch me."

*   *   *

Only five of them were selected for the trip. Bruno heard the sound of helicopter landing at the campus. It was time to leave. He saw Angela, Adams, Raj and Cheng chatting. Adams was telling new joke he had heard: a policeman stops a car by mistake and goes to apologize. But before he can do so, the driver says: "I'm sorry, officer, I forgot my license." His mother-in-law whispers from the backseat, "I told you, we would be caught in stolen car." Just then, the policeman hears a man's voice from the trunk: "Have we crossed the border?"

Everybody started laughing. Adams always told nice jokes. He had great fun with his friends at the castle; his muscular body was shaken with laughter. This happy moment was interrupted by the instructor.

The man in black suit gave a sign: it was time to get into helicopters. "Please wear these bracelets," the instructor asked. They looked like high-end jewelry; each one had a unique design.

"Yo, man. That's cool!" Adams shouted. "That's what I am talking about! This kind of bling goes with my style!"

The instructor said, "Adams, you're working with Angela and Bruno. Your legend is that you are an arms dealer and you have come to Monte Carlo for business negotiations. Here is your passport. Angela and Bruno, you will be Russian "*nouveau riche*" children. According to legend, your mother is Italian, she divorced your Russian father, and you spend your time between your homes in St. Petersburg and Venice. Take your passports. Cheng and Raj, you will be exchange students on holiday. You need to act like tourists on a strict budget. You'll arrive in the second helicopter. And as you might have guessed, we'll be spending tonight in Monaco," the instructor explained.

"Wow!" Raj shouted. "Finally, we are going to visit a cool place!"

"Your bracelets have built-in tracking devices," the instructor continued, "Don't try to remove them, in any situation, as we won't be able to find and help you."

"This sounds too good to be true," Angela thought, "You can just remove the bracelet and, finally . . . be free?"

The helicopter landed next to private French villa. The view was breathtaking. "Please get ready," the instructor said, "The car will take you to your hotel."

In the evening, Bruno saw Angela in red Valentino dress and Cartier necklace. Her long legs, gorgeous figure and beautiful smile fascinated him. She looked like a movie star or a Greek goddess. She was amazing.

"Wow, Bruno! Never thought you'd look so great in suit."

"Well, Angela, in that low cut dress, it will be you, not me, breaking hearts tonight," he said.

"Yo, ma peeps. You look cool," Adams said, opening the connecting door to the suite. "Adams himself looked more like weapons smuggler, not an arms dealer," Angela thought. His body was tough but his smile was charming and almost sweet. He had a heart of gold.

*   *   *

Raj and Cheng were upset. "Why can't I be the Maharaja of Jaipur tonight? Why do I have to be an exchange student on a budget?" Raj asked.

"Listen, guys. We're all part of something bigger than; who wears designer clothes, or who gets to stay at a fancy hotel. Everybody is doing important job. Raj, Cheng, you have to replace surveillance cameras," the instructor continued, "This is a crucial task for our safety. Don't think that you're not important."

"*Thik hei boss*–Will do, Sir," Raj said in Hindi. Cheng, kept quiet. He was extremely reserved and always focused. Cheng was one of the school's top students in martial arts. The school expected him to become an exceptional agent in the near future.

*   *   *

Angela and Bruno entered the famous Monte Carlo casino. The building in Art Nouveau style looked beautiful. It was favorite spot of global movers and shakers. The casino did not have the size of Venetian Macau or Singaporean Sentosa, but it definitely could boast of the glorious history. From the Hyderabadi Nizams to Russian Princes–the place was known for nobility guests. Bruno was amazed by what he saw: ladies in haute couture dresses, wearing necklaces worth of millions euros; gentlemen, smoking Cuban cigars and flashing Swiss limited edition watches. It was like being at James Bond movie set. But you are not the audience, but the star yourself. He saw the Prince of Monaco leaving the casino. Bruno almost felt high from the smell of champagne, perfume and cigars. Finally, he noticed the billionaire, who they had to befriend. The oligarch was taking straight shots of vodka and gambling big time.

"How you want to go about it?" Bruno asked Angela.

"Let's go to the bar and have a drink," she suggested. They ordered a bottle of champagne. "Now, Bruno, I will talk to a barman and you leave. Go and play."

Bruno placed the chips on 13, his lucky number. The roulette wheel started rolling. Some players leaned forward to watch the ball spinning; a few moments later it landed on a winning number.

"*Treize*–thirteen," the croupier said in French, nodding at Bruno. "Monsieur, s'il vous plait–Sir, please." The dealer passed winning chips to Bruno.

"*Ah, mais arrête toi!*–Come on, stop!" Angela shouted in French, "What are you doing? You promised you would not play roulette today!"

The billionaire stared at the girl, shifting his drink to the side. "*Kakaya krasotka!*–What a beauty!" the oligarch admired in Russian. Bruno understood her plan.

"No! I want to play," Bruno said.

"Then I am leaving to the bar," she shot back, "You want to lose like last time, Bruno? You are wasting father's money." Angela left. Bruno understood her plan.

"*Monsieur*, what is your decision? Do you want to play?" the dealer asked.

"No, cash out. She spoilt my mood . . . *Oh, les femmes!*–Oh, ladies!" Bruno came to the bar and shouted at Angela: "You . . . are you happy now? I am going to a restaurant and then home. I am tired of you behaving like my mother. Here," he said, throwing some chips at her. "Give the tip to whomever you want." Bruno left.

The Russian billionaire liked what he saw. He cashed out and moved to the bar. Angela acted as if she were very upset.

"*Devuskha!* No, that's Russian. How you say it in French? . . . *Oh, Mademoiselle,* what has happened?" the billionaire asked.

Angela looked at the oligarch. He was very handsome. His muscular body almost promised sinful pleasures. It was clear why all these beautiful models were after him. Vlad was the perfect catch: handsome, hot and super rich.

She asked the oligarch, "Did you say *'devuskha'*? You speak Russian?"

"*Da, konechno. A ty?*–Yes, of course. And you?" the oligarch asked in Russian.

"*Ya tozhe govoryu po russki,*–I also speak Russian," Angela replied. They switched into Russian. "My father is Russian and my mother is Italian."

"Who was that stupid guy without manners?" Vlad asked, "Your boyfriend?"

"No, that's my brother," Angela answered, "His name is Bruno." The billionaire smiled.

"My name is Vladimir, like Vladimir Putin. But of course, I am richer and more handsome than him," he smirked. Angela smiled back. "In fact, just call me Vlad. All my close friends call me Vlad." Angela's smile became even warmer.

"OK, Vlad. I'm Angela."

"I love your smile," Vlad said. "Such a pretty girl shouldn't be upset. Your smile is like sunshine."

"Thanks, Vlad."

"I want to give you a small gift," he said, placing a mobile in her hand. "Here, it's a Vertu phone with my private number. If you like me, you can call me." His grip was strong, but gentle at the same time. Angela thought, "Vlad must be a perfect in bed; he will, surely, be passionate and powerful, but also caring. The billionaire would give a girl the maximum pleasure. And with all of his traveling around the world, Vlad definitely has the technique of the ultimate global lover." Angela had no doubt that Vlad's innocent words: "If you like me, you can call me," actually suggested steamy love making sessions. This guy was dangerously hot, and he knew it.

"So sweet of you, Vlad. I should also give you a gift," Angela replied after a long pause.

"Angela, you have already given me a present. You smiled."

Angela put the phone in her clutch bag and stood up. "Vlad, I'm going to the ladies room. I'll be right back."

"Of course, Angela. I understand. You want to see your beautiful face in mirror and make it prettier. Total waste of time, but all girls that I know love makeup."

Angela closed the cabin door, she couldn't believe her luck. She took the Vertu phone out of her clutch bag. Fortunately, she was familiar with Symbian OS. Still, she had to hack fast. I just hope Mike is there, she thought. She managed to break the firewall, and then waited. She glanced nervously at her watch; only 3 minutes left before she gets caught.

"Cool dude. It's me, doll." These were secret code phrases. In case somebody hacked them, it would look like innocent flirting.

"Baby doll, you look great tonight."

"Even you look good, dude," she answered. "Great, it was Mike!" Angela thought.

"Dude, I have a used bracelet. Should I have it polished?"

"No way, doll! You'll die from a heart attack if you lose it."

"Thanks, cool dude."

"Take care of yourself, baby doll."

"Bye, dude," Angela answered. She deleted the browsing history and cache on the oligarch's phone.

"So, that's what it was!" Angela thought. The bracelet the instructor gave her wasn't meant to track her down and help her. It was designed to kill her if she tried to escape. Once again, she was trapped. Angela touched up her lipstick and came out of the bathroom. The Russian oligarch was still there. He looked happy when she came back.

"I'm sorry, Vlad, but I can't accept this phone. It's too expensive," Angela said.

"So you don't want to call me? You are the first girl in my life who wants to return a gift. Normally after the first gift, girls come back and ask for more. Anyway, Angela, I never take gifts back. If you don't like it, just throw the phone away. Actually, you are so different from other girls. I think . . . I should marry you. Yes! You will be the perfect wife!"

Angela was puzzled. She had heard a lot about Russian drinking and generosity, but this was the first time in her life she witnessed what many described as the "mystifying Russian soul."

Angela saw an angry Bruno, approaching the bar, "Who's that?" he shouted. "First, you act like my mother and then you behave like a cheap girl? Why are you sitting so close to some stranger? Our father should remove your name from the family trust."

The Russian oligarch became nervous. He obviously didn't expect this outburst, his bodyguards moved closer. Angela smiled, then laughed, as if she had had too much to drink and said: "He is not a stranger. His name is Vlad. He is a respectful businessman and he even told me that he would love to marry me. And as you know, Bruno, I am already 21. So don't talk to me as I were a child! I can marry Vlad right now!"

"Marry?" Did Bruno hear that right? "Well, Angela's hot body in this tight, low cut dress would make any drunk guy ready to marry her and start the honeymoon right away! The situation is very tricky. I should handle it without ruining the chance of friendship with oligarch," he thought.

Bruno smiled and said politely, "I am sorry. I've inherited hot temper from my mother. She is Italian. Nice meeting you, Vlad. My name is Bruno." The billionaire relaxed, and nodded at his bodyguards to sit down.

"OK, Bruno," Vlad said. "You are a real man. I am real a real man. Let's have drinks like real men." Bruno remembered that the instructor ordered them to get into the oligarch's villa at any cost. "Drinking would be the best excuse to start a new friendship," he thought at the time.

A few hours later, Bruno realized he should not have started drinking with the billionaire in the first place. Even though Vlad had already looked drunk, it didn't appear to count. They got a fresh bottle. The Russian oligarch started saying how there is no better vodka than Stolichnaya. He complained that black caviar could not compete with simple village herrings.

"Remember, Bruno, you can't buy real friends. Who are now my real friends? They all died, Bruno. All got killed. Now, I only pay. I have paid girlfriends, paid bodyguards, paid drivers, paid maids. No love, Bruno. You can't buy love! Remember, Bruno! Bruno, you are not drinking. Come on let's start." Not to blow his cover Bruno had to drink straight from the glass without lemon, ice, salt or food. It was crazy. After the first drink of vodka, he tried to grab some nuts. The

Russian billionaire stopped him saying in Russian, *"Posle pervoy ne zakusyvayout!*–After first drink you can't have food!"

"But I had champagne already," Bruno tried to argue.

"Champagne is for kids, Bruno. You are a real man. You have to drink vodka. *Monsieur*, repeat, please." Bruno stopped counting drinks.

The billionaire kept drinking and continued telling his life story: "I helped the president, the Russian president. I gave big money. But he has forgotten me now. Bruno, life is such a bitch. Sorry, beauty," he said to Angela, "Excuse my bad language." Angela continued drinking champagne.

"She is a sweet girl," oligarch said. "Bruno, real woman should never get drunk. Why, Bruno?"

Bruno really didn't know how to answer so he asked, "Why?"

The billionaire answered, "Because a real woman should bring her man home when he gets drunk. It is love, Bruno. Real love! You can't buy real love."

"It is boring here," the oligarch exclaimed after some time, "Let's go to my villa."

"Finally," Angela thought. Bruno and Vlad tried to stand up. It was not easy because they finished the whole bottle of vodka. The bodyguards tried to help them, but Russian billionaire shouted, "Don't touch me. *Ya trezv kak steklyshko!*–I am stone cold sober!" Bruno and Vlad hugged each other and made their way to exit. The bodyguards escorted them to the limo. In twenty minutes, they reached the oligarch's villa.

"Wow!" Angela thought, the villa looked breathtaking.

"The girl should go to sleep now," billionaire said.

"OK," agreed Angela. Vlad tried to kiss her on the lips to wish her good night, but Angela pushed him away, politely yet firmly.

Russian started laughing, "She is a pussy."

Bruno shouted, "How dare you!"

"No! Sorry, Bruno. Not pussy . . . pussy is a wrong word."

"Kitten?" Bruno asked.

"Yes, Bruno! Russian word is '*kochechka*,' English–'kitten'. That's a right word for Angela. She is all fluffy and cute, but has claws."

"Yes, she can scratch you," Bruno agreed.

"One more drink," the Russian shouted. "We should drink for '*Koshecka*,' the lovely kitten!"

The housekeeper showed Angela to one of the luxurious suites. Angela locked the door, and then checked the room for cameras. Not finding any, she removed her fancy shoes and stunning dress. She looked in the mirror. Her figure was perfect. Angela stepped into Jacuzzi; it was a nice, warm feeling. She thought about the billionaire. His eyes were so intoxicating, when they flirted tonight in the casino; but Vlad is a tough and dangerous guy. "What would he do to me if he found out that I had put spying devices in his home?" Angela decided not to think about Vlad. She took out her Vertu phone and switched it on. She managed to hack the firewall fast. Mike was near his tablet. He had a sixth sense that Angela would try to contact him again.

"Cool dude, it's me doll." She typed the secret code phrase.

"Baby doll, you look great tonight."

"Even you look good dude," Angela answered. "Nice! It was Mike," Angela relaxed.

"Dude, I got a mobile for free calls. You want to use?"

Mike could not believe his luck.

"Yes, doll, we can use it for the transfer." So many times he had those dreams that one day he would be able to move a few million dollars into offshore accounts. Finally, the future was secure. His hands were slightly shaking from the excitement. Angela saw the account number on the screen. In a few seconds, the transaction was complete.

"Bye, baby doll."

"Bye, cool dude."

Mike went to sleep, smiling happily after so many sad days. He was finally starting to believe that escape would be possible.

*　　*　　*

"Bruno, let me introduce you to my friends," the billionaire said. There was a big party happening near pool: models, politicians, actors, businessmen—the oligarch seemed to know everyone.

Bruno lost count of his drinks. After some time, the oligarch said, "Okay, Bruno my friend, please meet the gorgeous Russian singers—Masha and Dasha."

Bruno could hardly stand. The girls were drop dead gorgeous: next to them, Playboy playmates would look ordinary. Masha was platinum blond with huge boobs, and dressed in a tight short dress that left nothing to imagination. Dasha had curly black hair and deep blue eyes. Her legs were endless. The girls smiled when they saw Vlad, but their smiles became even warmer when they noticed Bruno.

"Bruno, you are so handsome! What muscles!" Masha cried, "Let me touch you!" Bruno was shocked. These girls were so open-minded and hot.

"Masha, enough! I want to touch Bruno now," Dasha said, pulling on Bruno's arm.

Vlad told him: "Bruno, my friend, I am going to sleep." Bruno hugged the Russian oligarch, and went to the pool area. Masha and Dasha followed him. The girls removed their clothes and jumped into the pool. "Aren't they hot?" Bruno overheard two guys talking to each other. "These babes are real bombshells–they are Russia's secret weapon," the Brazilian guy joked.

Masha and Dasha called Bruno, "Come here, chocolate boy. Let's enjoy." Bruno thought for a while and then jumped into the pool. The water was amazing.

The girls were smiling seductively, "Bruno, you should have one drink for our new friendship."

Bruno said, "No way. I've had enough for tonight, girls."

"Oh, OK. Can I get you mineral water?" Dasha asked.

"OK," Bruno agreed.

"One Perrier, please," Dasha ordered from a passing waiter.

Dasha handed Bruno a glass with sparkling water. Bruno finished his drink and told the girls, "Good night, Masha. Good night, Dasha."

The girls looked at him and giggled: "Bruno, don't be silly. We will show you to your room." He followed the girls upstairs. The housekeeper offered to help, but the girls answered, "No, it's fine. We'll escort him. That's your room, Bruno," they said, dropping him at the door.

Bruno stepped inside the room, and locked the door behind him. Dropping his clothes on the floor, he went straight into the shower. It was a long day–Bruno felt exhausted–he had drank too much. Finally, he fell asleep. He hardly had rest for an hour or so, when bright light woke him up. "Already morning?" wondered Bruno, opening his eyes. His hands and legs were handcuffed. "This can't be a good sign," Bruno thought, recalling the scenes of torture from his classroom videos. These could be his last hours.

Dasha and Masha were standing near him.

"What is it, girls?" he asked, trying to sound as normal as possible. The girls were still very high.

"Sorry, Bruno," Dasha smiled. "We are going to have a little fun . . . Why such a long face? Are you underage or what?"

"No, I am 22!" Bruno answered. "So these babes just want to have fun?" Bruno thought, feeling immediately relieved. "OK, Girls, untie me and let's have fun!"

"No, Bruno, we are not stupid," Masha giggled. "You are so strong. We can't untie you. We want to dominate you. We like to be girls on top," Dasha said, removing her bra and panties. She looked amazing. The Russian beauty took him straight to paradise. Masha smiled naughtily and joined Dasha. Both girls had the moves. Their body rhythm was synchronized. No wonder Vlad said that the singers performed well together. After some time Bruno shouted, "OK, girls, you had enough time. Now you can untie me."

"Bruno, don't be stupid," Dasha said, "We're just getting started."

"See, Dasha. It will take me some time to get ready for some action."

"That's okay. We're not in hurry," Masha purred.

"Bruno, you want some Perrier or juice?"

"Well, juice will be fine," Bruno answered. He had a glass of juice. Dasha started kissing him. Surprisingly, he was already ready. 'The drink?' Bruno wondered.

As if reading his mind, Masha said, "Sorry, Bruno, we put Viagra in your drink. We like to enjoy."

'These girls are nymphomaniacs!' Bruno thought. The girls kept singing in Russian: "*Muzhina moey mechty segodnya so mnoyu ty!*–My dream guy, tonight you are with me!" Bruno was shocked how much energy these girls had. "Dream guy? Do they mean I am the one? In that case . . . I just hope they will stop dreaming about me soon," Bruno thought. Finally, the Russian babes were done.

"Bruno, this is the key. Please take it and unlock yourself." The girls sent him flying kisses and ran from the room. Bruno unlocked himself. It was madness. He was practically dominated by these Russian babes.

The next morning, Bruno went for breakfast, even though he was still exhausted from last night.

Dasha and Masha were already there, smiling happily: "Hi, Bruno!"

Angela was also at breakfast, enjoying her Brazilian coffee, "Making new friends, huh?"

Bruno managed to give Angela a smile. His whole body was aching, and he still had a hard-on. 'How much Viagra these crazy babes put into my drink?' he wondered. He could have died from a heart attack.

"Where is Vlad?" Angela asked.

"Oh, he left for London . . . some urgent meeting," Masha answered.

Bruno said, "We also need to leave, Angela."

"We will come with you, Bruno."

"No, thanks, Masha!" Bruno answered.

Angela was surprised. Bruno normally would boast about all the pretty girls, dying to be in his arms. Why did he refuse to drop Russian babes? Maybe he was scared she would spoil his name in the castle.

"Come on, Bruno, we can give them a lift."

The girls laughed happily.

"In fact," Masha said, "we have our limo here. We will drop you guys. Where do you stay?"

"Hotel de Paris," Angela answered.

"Wow, that's nice one, we always book Churchill suite there. It is very cool place."

"Cool place?" Bruno thought, "Churchill suite will be around 10 k euro per night? These girls don't know better way to spend their money."

"All right, let's go," Dasha called the driver. Their limo was huge. The Russian babes dropped Angela and Bruno to the hotel.

"If you are free tonight, join us for a drink," Russian bombshells offered.

"Yes, I am dyeing to have drink with you tonight," Bruno seemed to be extremely frustrated. Angela and Bruno went back to their suite.

12 hours before

Adams left his suite at Hotel de Paris, he was about to give one of the best performances in his life.

Adams went down to the lobby, looked around. Well, here he comes–Mr. Frank Lucas–the famous arms dealer. Adams decided to act fast. He looked furious when he went to reception.

"Hey, man!" he shouted at reception desk. All people in the lobby looked at him. He stood out: 6'2 black guy–with huge muscles that his Versace t-shirt hardly covered. He looked straight out of a gangster movie. The American arms dealer Lucas stared at Adams.

"Hey, man, ain't stupid!" Adams shouted.

"*Monsieur*, what could I do for you?" the scared concierge asked.

"I ain't gonna stay at a 4 star hotel; my agent booked me at a 5 star deluxe. This ain't a 5 star, man! . . . only a 4 star!"

The American arms dealer Lucas laughed. It was hilarious.

"*Monsieur*, Monaco does not have a 5 star hotel. 4 star is highest rate of the hotels here; 5 star–was created by Americans. Our hotel is one of the most luxurious and prestigious in Monaco. It belongs to the Prince of Monaco. His Highness dined and stayed here."

"Bullsh.t, man. I ain't gonna lie I feel stupid, I ain't gonna stay a 4 star hotel. Check me out!"

"*Monsieur*, your nega . . ."

Adams hit reception desk with his huge fist, "What's the f..k? Did you just call me n..ger to my face?'

"No! No! No, *Monsieur*!" the concierge protested, "I was saying negative . . . negative impression of our hotel would change. Pardon, M*onsieur*, my Monegasque accent!"

"Nah man, it ain't like that," Adams shouted, he looked very angry and dangerous. Guests in the lobby were nervous. The situation escalated.

The dealer decided to help Adams. He came to the reception.

"Hey man, relax, no shit here a 4 star deluxe hotel here gonna be a 5 star–in states."

Adams looked back, turned around and then smiled. His smile was completely disarming.

"Hey, thanks bro. Finally, imma talk English. Got it, bro. Thanks, man, again."

"See ya, man. Gonna have drink if u're 'round," Lucas said.

The concierge protested, "*Monsieur*, but I was explaining same thing."

"Just shut it, man. You wanna spoil my mood again."

Adams left.

Lucas, the American arms dealer, went towards the lift. He didn't even notice that Adams managed to put a tracking device in his bag, while they were chatting.

"Yo, mission accomplished," Adams congratulated himself and went back to his suite.

*   *   *

Bruno went to take a shower. Suddenly, somebody knocked. Angela opened the door. Adams asked, "Doll, when did you come back? I got worried. You guys didn't show up last night. What happened?" Angela just managed to tell Adams about their visit to Russian oligarch's villa, when Bruno came out of the shower. His body wrapped in a towel looked hot. Even supermodel would kill for his bronzed, muscular torso and 6 pack abs.

"Hey, wassup, ma man?" Adams shouted. Angela realized that Adams and Bruno wanted to talk privately.

"I will go down to have some tea. You can join me later, guys."

"Yeah, sure we'll come, doll."

Angela left.

"Hey, Bruno, tell me ma man what happened?"

"These Russian babes were so bad."

"Why? Were they ugly chicks?" Adams asked.

"No way! They look better than Victoria Secret angels. But . . . They practically dominated me."

"Hey, what're you saying, man? It's just like a fantasy, right? Hot babes're dyeing to 've fun with you."

"Believe me, bro, they were hot but . . . hot as hell. They put a Viagra in my drink!" Adams started laughing. He was overjoyed.

"That's not all, Adams! These nymphomaniacs already stole my room card and they know I stay here."

"Hey, Bruno, do me a favor," Adams said. "Give me your room for tonight, if you don't mind, I will call Raj and Cheng. We will have the best night of our lives. What do you say, ma man?"

It was the first time Bruno smiled happily since yesterday afternoon. "I say 100 per cent yes. My room is yours."

Adams found Raj and Cheng in their tiny room at the Novotel hotel. The poor guys looked so upset.

"Well, Adams, it is just not fair. You, guys, enjoy so much and all we have is a budget version of Monaco. It is stupid, bro!"

"Yeah, ma man, I feel the same way. And in case you're not going to boast about it in the castle. I invite you to my suite at the Hotel de Paris."

"That's great!" Raj shouted, "Finally, we're getting justice."

"And if all goes well, I have a great surprise for you tonight . . . OK, Raj, Cheng, wear this stuff, I meet you at 11 pm sharp."

Raj and Cheng were extremely excited. Raj started singing in Hindi, "*Teri meri, meri teri prem kahani*–Mine, yours, yours, mine love story," then he said, "Hey, Cheng, I hope tonight I will meet a beautiful foreign girl. I will come to her and tell her, 'Hi, my name is Raj. It means *'prince'* in Hindi. Will you be my *'rani'*-princess?"

Cheng smiled, "It is very bad pick up line, Raj. But who knows . . . maybe you will get finally lucky and meet some girl."

"It should happen tonight, Cheng. Come on, I am 22, and still a virgin!" Raj answered.

10 hours later

Raj and Cheng entered rotating door of the famous Hotel de Paris and almost whistled. The luxury was outstanding: gold, marble, red carpets, the magnificent décor of belle époque.

"Cheng, today we are real *rajas* . . . in fact not *rajas*, bro, but *maha rajas*–the greatest kings!" Adams sent the butler, who escorted Raj and Cheng to the suite. Bruno couldn't stop smiling. The Russian babes will get the lesson of their life tonight!

At exactly 1 am the door got opened. Bruno slept peaceably in his bed. The girls began crawling towards him.

"Our chocolate boy is right here," Dasha whispered.

"So cute," Masha added.

Just before the girls reached his bed, the lights were switched on . . . Adams, Cheng and Raj stepped out of the darkness into the light and surrounded the girls. But there were three girls.

"Who are you?" Bruno asked.

"I am Natasha, I am Russian supermodel, I am friend of Dasha and Masha," the brown hair babe with huge boobs answered.

"It is just a perfect night," Raj thought.

"Well, ladies, I hope you will have a great time," Bruno said and left the suite.

It was definitely triumph for boys. The girls looked shocked. The guys were totally happy. "Well, unlike you ladies we don't believe in handcuffs." They moved closer to girls.

The night was fantastic. The girls left happy and satisfied in the morning, leaving behind them the smell of French perfume and seduction. Monaco was mesmerizing.

CHAPTER 2

LEARNING THE GANSTER SLANG

Angela was not happy to be back to castle. Monaco made her realize how much she wanted to be free and live life on her own terms. She finished her breakfast, Mike was not there. Angela missed Mike. He was the only person whom she could trust. She looked at her watch. The Hindi language class was about to start.

Each agent at the castle had to speak at least 5 languages. Accent was extremely important. The class was full. Two Indian guys: Anil and Raj were chatting in the corner. Most of students were horrified by the Hindi language professor. He got a nickname "Monster". Professor used to mock cruelly his students. Many of the girls would burst into tears after his disgusting remarks. Mr. Kumar entered the class and brought the feeling of fear with him, the students stopped talking immediately.

"*Namaste,*–hello," Mr. Kumar said in Hindi, "Today, we will first repeat the pronunciation of long 'aa' and short 'a' and then we will study the language of Mumbai (Bombay) underworld: the famous *tapori* slang. Please switch on your tablets. OK, James, please tell us in Hindi–I am going away."

James could hardly pick up Hindi.

He said, *"Mein ja raha hoon."* Each student tablet showed on display: *"Mein ja raha hoon."*–the software had voice recognition system.

"Is it correct, James? Are you sure that it is *ja'* and not *jaa'*? Stand up, young man!" James looked confused. Mr. Kumar got angry: "You, idiot, how many times I have to tell you it is *jaa'* not short *ja'*?" James got really embarrassed; he tried not to look at his friends.

"Raj, what do you think?"

"It is *jaa'*, Sir."

"See, James not everybody is fool like you. Sit down, Raj. Well, class, now we will study tapori language–the famous underworld slang. I will teach you how to swear better than local gangsters."

Angela plunged in her thought. She wanted to find out how to break the firewall. Professor Kumar noticed her absent look. "All right, class, in *tapori* slang we call a girl *'chickni'*."

"That's not *tapori!*" Adams, well built black guy, shouted. "It is American African gangster language–and now, cool guys like me, use it. We call the girls *'chick'*. These Mumbai gangsters must have stolen it is from us," Adams ended with a proud smile.

"Just shut up, Adams! It is not copied. It is *'chikni'* not 'chick'. Alright, class, in tapori language there is high usage of 're': *'kya re'?*–what is it? *'arre'*–hey."

Adams interrupted again, "Sir, they took this style also from us, we add 'yo' to sound cool."

"Adams!" Monster shouted, "One more remark and I will throw you out of class."

Professor Kumar looked at Angela again. "So, Angela, if I were tapori gangster, I would call you *'chikni*–hot babe' and I would tell you: *'Kya re chikni!*–What a hot babe!'," Mr. Kumar said with disgusting sleazy smile.

Angela looked at the "Monster" and replied, *"Arre ! Apunko malum hei hum chikni hei–aur tere ko kya lagta hei, tu bhai hei? Ben ch.d . . . kuta, kamina, saala tu hi hei!"* There was silence in the classroom: except Anil and Raj, nobody understood what Angela said. The "Monster" got red with embarrassment. It was first time anybody saw him like that.

Anil and Raj were laughing so much that Raj fell from his chair. *"Tu cheez badi hei mast, mast!*–You are great!" they sang in Hindi. Everyone started typing in their tablets, "What did she say?"

Anil wrote to everyone: Angela said, "Hey, I know I am sexy doll. U gonna think, you're the don? You're mother f.cker ! Dirty dog, son of bitch, that's who u're."

Mr. Kumar finally managed to calm down: "Class, start reading exercise no 23." The bell rang. Mr. Kumar rushed out of the classroom.

"Hey, Angela, you made my day," James said, "Thanks, babe!"

Adams came to Angela, "Yo, doll, u're super today!"

Anil and Raj shouted "*Tu cheez bari hei mast, mast!*–You are great!" Bruno looked at Angela. "Strange," he thought, "Angela is really sweet girl". He always felt that Angela was more into her own world.

The beauty, who just gets it all, for herself. She would never stand up for somebody else.

"You did great, Angela. I wish I had guts to put 'Monster' earlier in his place. I am proud of you. You can count on me." Angela looked deeply into Bruno's eyes. The beauty of her eyes was simply breathtaking.

"Maybe, I can trust him?" she thought for a second, "No! The risk is too high."

"Thanks, Bruno," Angela said and left the classroom. Bruno went back to his room. He had a break before driving lesson class. He remembered Angela's eyes again and again. It seemed for a moment that she wanted to open the door to her secret inner world. "No! I must be imagining things," Bruno thought and started doing his homework.

CHAPTER 3

ALEXANDER: THE GREEK GOD

The boy turned his striking blue eyes towards the teacher: "The solution exists, but the file needs to be converted into binary mode."

Professor Goldman decided to check . . . "Yes, it works. This boy is a genius! We never had anyone like him. He has no limit. He can reach any level . . . and even higher than the level we, professors, can imagine because unfortunately our imagination is limited," Professor Goldman thought.

The boy's face and body belonged to a Greek God, not human being. His facial and body features were so perfect and symmetrical that it felt scary, almost creepy to be near him. He didn't look normal; he was extraordinary. The boy just turned 21. However, most of his life he spent alone. The boy was isolated from other kids at the age of 9. Professors noticed that any class slowed him down. The boy had a photographic memory: he enjoyed quoting works of Plato and Aristotle in ancient Greek. He loved reading

Shakespeare plays and reciting poems of Goethe in German. When solving complicated mathematical equations, he used to listen to Mozart and Beethoven. The boy was highly intellectual, but very old fashioned. When he was asked if he liked trance, rap, house music or MTV shows; he would answer he did not like any of the above mentioned as they lacked systematic order and structure.

The group of professors and doctors were examining latest video of the boy.

"Mr. Goldman," Moriarty, professor of psychology, looked again at the monitor, "I believe that the boy is severely depressed. You need to integrate him immediately into a social group."

"What do you suggest colleagues?" Professor Goldman asked the group of doctors.

"In last few months the boy started having recurring headaches," Dr. Nelson reported.

"I believe colleagues we need to give the boy some rest. I know that the class will slow him down, but the boy will not be able to survive in isolation. The depression will progress and his condition will worsen very soon," Professor Moriarty explained.

After long discussions, the decision was made: they boy will be sent to the castle. He was taken by private jet.

CHAPTER 4

HACKING

The computer class was about to start, everybody adored Professor Zelikman. He was genius. Mr. Zelikman was friendly and funny; he behaved more like a friend than supervisor.

"Hello, guys!"

"Hello, Professor Zelikman."

"Today we need to revise what we have learnt last week and then I will teach you new stuff. Yes, my friends, as you may have guessed today you will hack the system. I hope you will love it, guys."

Mike was getting impatient. He was waiting for Professor Zelikman finally to give the order to hack into the system.

"OK, guys, so let's learn new stuff. Our goal today is to hack the system of big organization. Well, if you want to hack the system of the large organization, such as bank, government institution, hospital etc . . . you have several options to do it.

The first one is to create your own hacking device. Remember, your device needs to be very powerful, so that it could detect common patterns of letters and numbers at high speed. Obviously, it will take serious effort to create one.

The other way is to create your link and send it to users. Basically, when the employees of a bank, a hospital or a government institution will click on your link, they will inadvertently start your program on their computers. This method has limitations because users have become smarter. Now, they know that it is dangerous to open unknown links. The good old time when innocent users would click stuff like: "I Love You", "230 Dead as Storm Batters the Europe" or "Anna Kournikova" is ancient history.

And of course, the third method is for those of you who were not lazy and managed to learn properly the programming languages. You guys can actually find the bugs in the original program and integrate your code into it. Then it is just a piece of cake. You make yourself administrator and then, you my friends, are in charge of the program!

Well, enough of theory, guys. Lets starts hacking the system! To make it more interesting I am giving 1000 euro to the one who breaks in first. You have 6 minutes–that is 360 seconds."

Mike looked at Angela. She knew that he wanted her to catch the IP address of the bosses.

"Your time starts now!" the professor shouted, clicking the virtual timer.

"OK, all these are our school IPs," Angela thought as she continued hacking through the system, "but that one clearly didn't belong here. Somebody tried to protect students from getting caught." Angela managed to find out that the foreign IP was not from Europe. It was from Middle East. "Not bad," she concluded, "at least it's a start."

"61, 62, 63 . . . ," the professor continued to countdown.

Angela remembered what Mike told her, "We should always be number three or four, but never number one, otherwise they will start to view as a threat and will track your each and every move. They will also install higher than normal standard firewall on your tablet."

The new boy was really good. Angela was waiting. She could get the prize but what she wanted was not 1000 euro. She wanted freedom!

"210 . . . 220 !" Mike was waiting as well. "350! OK, I got the winner."

The class looked surprised. The winner was a new guy.

"Your name, please."

"Alexander."

"OK, Alex, please come and collect your prize money." Professor Zelikman handed over two 500 euro notes.

"With all my due respect, Sir, I am here to serve my country and not to get gift . . . I will not accept this money. It is my duty to study well . . . and my name is Alexander. Alex is for small children." The bell rang. Alex took his tablet and left. There was silence in the classroom.

"He is definitely different," Professor Zelikman thought, as Alex took his tablet and left the room.

*   *   *

"What does he think of himself?" Bipasha shouted. "Mike, this new kid is not better than us. Just because he looks like a Greek god doesn't give him right to tell us what is right and what is wrong. All of us here want to serve our country. He has too much attitude . . . Mike, are you listening to me?"

Mike nodded.

"I really hate this new guy."

"I don't know Bipasha . . . How can I judge him? I just met him . . ."

*   *   *

"So what is happening with Alex? Is he integrated well?" Professor Wells asked.

"I would not say so, Professor Wells. Just have a look at this video," Professor Moriarty answered.

"How sad," Professor Goldman exclaimed, "I thought it would be good idea to bring him here. It seems I was wrong . . . I can't give up on this boy. We need to find solution. The boy is just so talented. We can't lose him."

"I agree," Professor Wells said, "I think we need to go back to his basic psychological profile. We must have missed something."

*   *   *

Angela went back to her room. She had to tell Mike about IP address.

"Cool Dude, it's me doll." She typed the secret code phrase.

"Baby Doll, you look great tonite."

"Even you look good, dude", Angela typed.

"Give me your 'I', doll."

"Oh, dude, I am not in mood for disco."

"I got it. You want to go on a vacation?"

"Yes, let's go to Middle East, dude."

"Any specific country, baby doll?"

"Not sure, cool dude."

"OK, baby doll."

"Bye, dude."

"Well," Mike thought, "at least we know now that the IP address belongs to Middle East. Not bad at all. We are coming closer."

CHAPTER 5

THE NEW KID ON THE BLOCK

Bipasha came for dinner to canteen. Mike saw her entering. Again his heart skipped a beat. She was so beautiful: tall, dusky, long silky black hair, big brown eyes. Mike was not sure that she will not laugh at him, if he told her about his feelings. Bipasha was Indian girl. Indian girls normally don't like '*goras*' (Caucasian foreigners in Hindi). They think goras are just here to have fun and don't know about true love. Bipasha saw Mike looking at her. She gave him a mesmerizing smile.

"*Hey, Mike, keyse hei*–How are you?" she asked in Hindi.

"*Mein acha hoon,*–I am fine," Mike answered.

"This new *gora* is totally fake. I just hate him. He threw so much attitude at Mr. Zelikman. What does he think of himself?" Mike tried to give her signs to speak quietly; she did not notice Alex was standing behind her.

Alex came to her and told her, "If you were a man I would challenge you to a duel for insulting me, but as you are a lady I would just prefer you tell me in the face what you think of me and not behind my back."

Bipasha was shocked; she didn't know what to say. Alex finished his juice and left canteen. He lost his appetite. Bipasha finally managed to overcome her shock and said: "Mike, I told you he has an attitude . . . I was wrong. He is a lunatic . . . Duel? What century is he living in?"

"Just forget him, Bipasha. You know you look so hot when you are angry."

"Hey, Mike, don't try to flirt with me. I will beat you with my shoe."

"I bet you will, Bips, you got black belt just recently in karate." Bipasha laughed happily. She enjoyed Mike's company. He was not like other *goras* in the school.

* * *

Alex just wanted to go back to his room and be alone. He could not understand this new world. The kids here were so cruel and double faced. They were not noble like heroes in his favorite books. He put Mozart on and started doing homework on his tablet.

* * *

Angela entered the canteen. She saw Bipasha and Mike chatting. She joined them. "Angela, what do you think of new *Greek God*?"

Angela looked surprised: "Whom?"

"Alex," Mike explained. Bips gave him this nick name. "Personally, I think I am handsome too," he smiled.

"Of course, you are," Bipasha agreed, "but your looks are pleasant. His beauty is too perfect as if he is . . . a sculpture, not a human being!"

"I don't know," Angela said, "I think he actually meant what he said . . . He is talented and smart. OK . . . maybe old fashioned would be the right word."

"Enough of diplomacy!" Bipasha interrupted, "He is a lunatic!" Bipasha left the canteen.

"I think I cracked the code," Mike said fast, turning away from camera. "I can stop the laser beams finally; you want to try to climb tonite?"

"Wow! That's great Mike. Of course, I want to try. Will you miss me if I escape tonight?"

"Of course, doll, you are the only person I can trust with my life here. I will send you message when it will be a safe timing."

"OK, cool, Mike . . . I will miss you too."

"I know, doll!"

"Mike, I never saw Deepika and Max again. I think it is strange."

"Something fishy is going on here, Angela. I mean so many of our friends just disappeared. We should try to find out what is really happening at the castle. Anyway, I have to leave now. See you later, Angela"

"Bye, Mike". They both left canteen

Angela was called to the professor's room "I just hope they don't know we I am trying to escape tonight," Angela thought. Professors and doctors were all sitting and watching Alex on large screen.

"My dear Angela," Professor Wells started, "As you know you were selected from millions of kids to serve your country. You possess amazing qualities. You are smart, beautiful young lady."

"OK, cool . . . They didn't find out," Angela relaxed.

"As you may have also guessed, though are very talented, there are kids more talented than you in the programming class."

"Well, I actually manage to hack your system. As for other students . . . Mike and me we are the best, but we can't tell you that," Angela thought.

"Look at the screen, this guy Alex is the best in programming at the castle, but as you may have noticed other students are jealous of him."

"You mean–Bipasha," Angela guessed.

"We have noticed that you have a generous heart and you accept his superiority without getting angry."

"That's really too much!" Angela was getting angry, "I am better than him: I cracked the code in 60 seconds he did in–350," she thought.

"Well, having analyzed his psychological profile, we found out that you are the perfect candidate to become his friend."

"I just hope not a girlfriend!" Angela thought. Last time when a guy tried to touch her booty: she didn't hesitate for a second and broke his wrist. It was a pleasant memory, and Angela smiled sweetly at the recollection.

Professor Wells, reading the signs differently and thinking of himself as extremely intelligent human being pronounced, "You see, Angela, your body language said it all. What we ask you is to help Alex to get integrated into campus community."

"Of course, Professor Wells, I will do that," Angela said and left the room.

"She is not the best student around but can be easily manipulated and definitely the most beautiful girl and she has that . . . sex appeal," Professor Wells said.

"I absolutely agree, Professor Wells! Colleagues, we made a perfect choice," Professor Goldman concluded.

CHAPTER 6

CAN I TRUST HIM?

Angela went to her room. At 11.00 pm sharp she got a confirmation from Mike: "You have 15 minutes, baby doll."

"OK, dude," Angela typed hurriedly. She rushed to the open air yard. The moon was full, she had to climb fast! Finally, the laser beams: she threw stone–it worked, the system was off! Now she needs to count each second. She put the timer on her watch and started climbing. She managed to get almost to the top of the hill. One more step . . . Some six sense stopped her. She threw the stone, lying near her feet, and it disappeared. The next row of laser beams was right there! It means they need to hack so many new codes. She felt miserable. Suddenly Angela saw some shadow. She started running. Angela jumped hurriedly; she was back in the campus yard. Alex entered. Angela recognized his shirt from far. The first thought was: "Did he see me?"–the second one–"If he saw me, would he tell others?" Angela decided to act naturally.

Alex was completely lost in his thoughts; he was surprised to see somebody in the darkness. It was too far. He could not see the face clearly. The girl's figure looked stunning in the moonlight. Her long golden hair was open. She was just like a vision from his novels: some beautiful mysterious stranger. Finally, he could see her face properly. It was the girl from today's computer class. Her eyes were amazing and lips were smiling. It seems like she also recognized him.

"Hey, Alex, what's up?" Her voice was like a sweet music. "Sorry, I mean Alexander." Nobody normally talked to Alex except professors and imaginary friends.

"I would like to apologize; I was not introduced to you Miss . . ."

"I am Angela."

"Very nice meeting you, Miss Angela."

"Well," Angela thought, "if he is to become my friend I will need to teach him how to speak properly. The way he speaks English sucks!"

"I had a severe headache, so I decided to make a small promenade. What a pleasant coincidence that you Miss Angela is here."

"Alex, you don't need to say Miss Angela. You can just call me Angela."

"But would not it be rude?"

"No, Alex, it sounds ruder to me if you say Miss every time. I mean none of my friends calls me Miss Angela."

"You think one fine day you could become my friend?"

"Why not Alex? Can I call you Alex and not Alexander? Alexander sounds too long."

"Yes, Miss . . . I mean, yes, Angela."

"You seem to be nice guy Alex." Alex felt so shy; no girl has complimented him ever.

"I don't know I felt very unwanted here."

Angela decided to change the topic, "What about your headache, when did it start?"

"Last month I tried to solve for a few days very sophisticated mathematical problem, I listened to Mozart as usual–as it relaxes my mind ("Mozart . . . Are you kidding me?" Angela thought) and that was the first time when it happened. I read Goethe poems after that, but it did not help ("Goethe . . . Is it for real?" Angela couldn't believe what she just heard)

"Alex, I feel your life became boring. You need an adventure. Tell me something . . . Do you trust me?"

Alex looked for a second in her eyes and then said, "Yes, Angela. I do."

"Then give me your hand." Angela took his hand. Alex felt great: such a beautiful girl holds his hand. "And now let's jump."

"Jump?" Alex looked shocked. He doubted just a second and then they jumped together. It was amazing feeling. They started climbing the mountain.

"OK, now we need to go back," Angela said.

"But why?" Alex asked, "This journey just started."

Angela thought, "To tell him or not? Can I trust him?" But somehow she had a gut feeling: she could trust this new boy. "You have to promise me it will be our secret."

"I swear, Angela, I will not tell anyone."

"Well, we can't cross here. Just check this out," she threw small stone.

"Are these laser beams?" the boy whispered, "But I am sure you can switch them off. You just need password."

"Alex, that's not all. There are hidden cameras everywhere. They record all what is happening here . . . and your tablet is always checked by supervisors."

"Angela, they told us that we can leave school any time we want. So how comes they put laser beams right here? Are these barriers to protect us or make us prisoners? What do you think, Angela?"

"Alex, I don't know, but you need to be very careful. I myself don't know the truth."

They jumped off the hill. Alex was feeling so happy and relaxed.

"Angela, you know I really want to become your friend. You are such a nice girl."

"You are also nice guy, Alex . . . but you need to learn how to speak like a modern boy. Otherwise students will just not accept you."

"Oh . . . OK, Angela, I will do my best."

"Bye, Alex."

"Bye, Angela."

Alex went to bed; he couldn't stop dreaming about the girl with golden hair, blue eyes and the sweetest smile. She was amazing. He remembered how she held his hand. It was magical.

Next morning professors were analyzing Alex's behavior. He entered canteen and looked happy. He switched on his tablet and started reading article on American slang. "Angela was right," Alex thought, "I need to be accepted here. I need to learn fast." It was clear Alex was waiting for somebody.

"Hey what's up, doll?" Alex said, trying to sound normal.

"Hey, Alex. All is cool. You make progress, Alex. I like how you speak now!"

Alex got red.

Bipasha entered the room. She felt awkward.

"Hey, Bipasha, I am sorry girl. I just had a bad day yesterday. I hope we are cool now?" Alex shouted.

Bipasha looked shocked, "Whatever . . . I just hope you are not bipolar," the girl mumbled.

"Just give her some time, Alex. She will be fine," Angela said. Mike entered canteen, Angela came near him and moved away from camera, "They have second row of beams, Mike."

"Shit . . . I thought we were so close," Mike said.

"I am trying to make Alex part of our team."

"Angela, are you mad? We can't trust him! He is new kid. Let's check him out first."

"You know yourself, Mike, we're moving too slowly. We need one more person: we can't do it on our own. We have to take the risk."

CHAPTER 7

WILL YOU DANCE WITH ME?

The dancing class started.

"All right, class, today I am going to teach you ballroom dancing," Mr. Blanc said. In the near future you will need to mix with powerful and influential people, who were brought up by best tutors and attended prestigious private schools. So, besides being intelligent and presentable, you will need to posses basic dance skills. OK, so ball room dancing is all about class, grace and elegance. It should not be too hot, so girls please don't shake your boobs like in belly dancing and don't move hips like in rumba. Plus, you should feel your partner and always dance as a couple.

Especially for Angela I repeat, young lady, you should not break your dance partner's hand when he holds onto your waistline." All the students laughed. Last time when Harun was her dance partner and slipped his hand onto her bottom; Angela didn't hesitate for a second and just broke the guy's wrist.

It became famous story in agents' school. "OK, Gentlemen, please invite the ladies."

Alex approached Angela immediately.

"Would I have the pleasure of dancing with you, gorgeous stranger?"

"Yes," smiled Angela.

"I hope you will not break my hand?"

"Let's see."

"Well, at least you didn't break my heart because you accepted my dance invitation."

"You are smooth operator, Alex!"

Alex smiled.

"One, two, three . . . One, two, three . . . ," *Maitre de danse* kept repeating. Steps were quite easy; after learning such complicated karate moves, remembering dance steps seemed to be a piece of cake. Mr. Blanc was impressed. Everybody made great progress. "Very good, class, very good!" After a few more minutes Maitre de danse started polishing up their dance moves:

"Adams, your body is too flexible. Hold your posture! It is not hip hop routine. Bipasha, why you are shaking your hips? It is not Bollywood style! Mike, what's wrong with you? I said the hand should be on the waist? Why you are touching Bipasha's booty? I mean, I know why . . . She has a great bum. But remember, Mike, none of respected ladies would allow you to do that in public. She will slap you, security will throw you from the ball room and your secret mission will be over. Come on, guys! Concentrate. One, two, three . . . One, two, three . . . Cheng, please look at lady's eyes, not at your shoes. You should impress your lady. What will she think? He likes to look at his shoes more than my face? No pretty lady will take that as a compliment. One, two, three . . . Very good! Continue."

The music got over. Some guys left their partners and went to get soft drinks and mineral water. The *Maître de danse* got frustrated, "*Non! Non! Non ! Mais ça . . . Ça ne marche pas!* It is just not working out! (When Mr. Blanc was emotional: he would switch to French–his native language) What's wrong with you, guys? Who leaves a lady like that? You have to thank her for dance and offer her drink. That's awful what you did, guys. No manners!"

Alex looked straight into Angela's eyes, kissed her hand and said, "*Mademoiselle, merci beaucoup* for your dance."

"*Ça . . . C'est parfait!–It is perfect!*" Mr. Blanc smiled. "*Mon cher ami,* your name please?"

"Alex".

"*Voila, Monsieur* Alex is very classy gentleman. That's the way to treat a lady." Mr. Blanc was really happy with Alex. The bell rang. The dancing class got over.

CHAPTER 8

WHITE NIGHT ROMANCE

Alex entered the room, "OK, my boy, please have a seat."

"A glass of water?"

"No thank you, Sir."

"OK, so my boy, what did you decide?" Professor Goldman asked. "Alex, are you ready to kill the president? This person caused a lot of pain to his people: his men raped underage girls, murdered innocent citizens without trial. He is evil and you, my boy, must be the hero and destroy the evil. You need to kill him."

"With all my due respect, Sir. I am sure we can find some other way. Killing is not a solution."

"You need to do it, Alex. It is my order. You are the agent and you have to follow the order!" Professor Goldman shouted.

"Sir, each agent must have moral conspicuousness, take the example of Hague tribunal dealing with war crimes. Those soldiers also followed orders of their officers, but now the soldiers are considered criminals, not heroes . . . I don't want to become like them, Sir."

"Alex, I am tired of your arguments, you are over-analyzing."

"Professor, can I ask you out for a minute?" the assistant said.

"OK!" Mr. Goldman looked totally frustrated, "This stupid boy is not going to follow the orders! Alex is about to become useless to us; he is like a high tech computer that keeps hanging instead of solving problems."

Mr. Goldman entered the professor's room.

"Look here please, Professor Goldman. Based on Alex's psychological profile, there is 99.9 per cent chance that after falling in love with a virgin girl and being her first man, Alex will follow the order to kill, in case he needs to save the girl's life."

"That's great news," Professor Goldman smiled. "Let's go for it."

*   *   *

"Angela and Alex, get ready the plane will pick you up in 3 hours," the instructor announced. They rushed packing. Angela and Alex were supposed to be young couple. According to the legend Alex was Greek, who fell in love with Angela (half Russian half Italian girl) and accompanied Angela to her home city. St. Petersburg in summer was even more romantic than Paris. Alex was under impression that Moscow was the best city in Russia. But coming to St Petersburg, he realized how wrong he was. In fact, except Red square, Moscow had nothing to shout about. St.

Petersburg had the most amazing Baroque and Rococo architecture. Huge number of colorful palaces, gold of cathedrals, splendid gardens with marble sculptors of Greek gods–everything fascinated Alex. The city was built on a grand scale–no wonder it was real Imperial jewel–home for Russian tsars for over 300 hundred years. And of course, St. Petersburg had white nights: the sunset was actually around midnight! It almost felt like the city wanted to give more time to enjoy its splendid beauty. Alex was charmed by St. Petersburg.

Alex and Angela had suite in 5 star deluxe Grand Hotel Europe: the oldest and most famous hotel in the city. White marble, gold, chandeliers, and Russian empire style–all was impressive here. Alex was so happy. The atmosphere was totally romantic; warm weather, white nights, flowers blossom, birds singing, young couples kiss and hug right on the streets of the fascinating city.

"Alex, isn't it ironic that James Bond movie was shot here?"

"Yeah, it is, Angela. We have to get ready. The car will come soon"

"OK, Alex."

The car took them to the most famous club of St. Petersburg. It was full. The girls were so beautiful here: tall, endless legs, long silky hair, amazing smiles. They all looked like supermodels. Well, Russia was always famous for beautiful girls. Russians joke that there are less waves in the Baltic Sea than beauties in St Petersburg. Angela and Alex noticed the oligarch. He was surrounded by bodyguards and exotic beauties: Chinese, African and Brazilian babes.

"Ladies and gentlemen," the anchor said, "Tonight we have something very special. We will have singing competition. And the prize will be worth of 100 K euro–courtesy of our great friend billionaire Vlad. The winner will get our beautiful prize: bottle made of pure gold with real Russian vodka.

"That's our chance, Angela, to get noticed by the oligarch."

"Actually, Alex, I don't sing well."

"But I do."

"Really? You never told me about it Alex."

"OK, so who wants to be the first contestant? Come on. Yes, young lady. Let's welcome her," the anchor asked. Everybody applauded. Unfortunately the girl only had great looks but she could neither sing nor dance. The crowd booed of disappointment.

"All right, now please welcome from Brazil hot model Giselle!" the anchor continued. Giselle could dance, but singing was not her strong point. The contestants kept coming and going, but none of them could sing well.

"All right, anybody else? Come on! What happened to you, guys? I repeat 100 K euro prize for the winner!!!"

Alex told Angela, "OK, now is the right time to come on stage."

"Best of luck, Alex."

"Thanks, Angela".

Alex came on stage, he caught a spotlight. The gay guy, sitting next to Angela shouted, "I am seeing an angel. Who is he? So handsome . . . so handsome, I want to cry now! How can anybody be so handsome?"

"Hi, my name is Alex and I would like to sing for you French song. It is not new song, but I hope this song will open heart of one beautiful girl and tonight will be the beginning of new love story." He started singing. His voice sounded amazing: "*Es si tu n'existais pas. J'assaierais d'invinter l'amour*–If you did not exist, I would have to create love."

"Who is he?" people started whispering, "He is too good! He has full package: voice, looks and talent."

Girls started recording Alex on mobiles. When Alex finished singing the club got mad. Some of the guests were shouting, "*Bravo*". Some demanded in Russian, "*Ezhe! Ezhe!*–Once more! Once more!" He became a star.

The fat old producer–Dima–asked his friend, "Did you record him?"

"Yes, Dima, I did. The boy is star material, man!"

"Cool, send me his video. Who is this Alex, anyway? Can he sing in Russian? I want to get to know him," Dima said.

Girls surrounded Alex and started chatting and flirting with him. In this club girls knew you have to be the first to catch the tomorrow's superstar. And there was no doubt this boy will become Russian megastar.

"Listen, babes, I am already with someone," Alex said, when Masha and Dasha asked him for his mobile number.

Russian bombshells checked Angela out. "I don't know what he found in her? Just an average beauty . . . Nothing special. These boys are mad. They always choose the worst girls," blond singer Masha said to her friend Dasha.

Alex came to Angela, "Can I get you new drink?"

"No thanks, Alex, I am still finishing this one. You became star Alex. You have it in you."

"Come on, Angela."

"I am serious Alex."

"All right," the anchor said, "Anybody else wants to try luck? Anyone? So who do you think will be the winner? You have to decide, guys!"

"Alex! Alex! Alex!" the crowd shouted.

"OK, guys, you chose your winner. Mr. Mysterious Alex, please come to the stage. Now, I would like to ask our special guest of honor and my dear friend Vlad to give you the prize. I remind you guys that it is bottle with real vodka inside made of gold. It is worth of 100 K euro!"

Alex took the microphone. "I would like to thank everyone and please bring glasses on stage." The oligarch came on stage and gave Alex golden bottle of vodka. Alex took the glass and offered first drink to the oligarch.

"You are sweet boy, you have good manners," the oligarch laughed.

"My first toast will be for the special someone in our lives", Alex continued, "Each of us has that special person in our lives. Cheers!"

"Cheers!" the crowd shouted. Everybody started drinking.

"You leave me your contacts, boy," oligarch Vlad requested, "My friend Dima wants to sign you."

"Yes sure, Sir."

"You can call me, Vlad."

"Thanks, Vlad."

"We hit the jackpot, Angela, the oligarch wants to talk to me. Let's come to their table." They went to the table of oligarch.

"What a babe!" fat producer shouted, "She is so hot!" Producer saw the ice in Alex's eyes.

"I am just joking, my friend. Hah Hah . . . I understand she is the special someone, right? First drink was for her, huh?" Dima asked. Alex nodded. "Alex, my boy, the best girls are always taken . . . you practically need to pick them from kindergarten and watch them. Only high class wh.res are always for sale. Anyway, can you sing in Russian?"

"Yes, Sir."

"Actually, Alex, don't call me 'Sir'. 'Sir' makes me feel too old. Call me Dima," fat producer asked. "Well, my boy, you have great talent, but you need right connections to become superstar. You can't do it on your own. So, Alex, you want to sign contract with us? We are the best in the business. You can check with anyone."

"I will need to think it over, Dima."

"OK, Alex, but don't think too long. We can offer you 1 million euro per year. Plus, you get 30 per cent from corporate events, marriages and concerts."

"I am very flattered, Dima, and will give you answer next week."

"You can put your girl in the video also . . . or girls."

"I would prefer one girl, Dima".

Handsome and muscular oligarch was talking to exotic models Gizele and Isabella. Suddenly he looked at Angela. His eyes were intoxicating: they almost promised forbidden pleasures.

"You are, Angela, right? You remember you came to my party in Monaco and stayed at my home?" Alex was not happy at all.

"Yes, Vlad, I remember."

"Yes, Angela, my kitten I wanted to marry you that night." The producer looked nervous. Alex could hardly control himself. "Anyway, Angela . . . so now you are with this . . . boy?" the oligarch laughed. Alex relaxed.

Oligarch started chatting again with Gizelle and Isabella.

In half an hour Angela and Alex decided to leave the party. The cab took them back to the hotel. Alex and Angela entered the suite.

"So what is that story with you and the oligarch?" Alex asked.

"Are you jealous, Alex?"

"Angela, I swear I felt like killing Vlad."

"Nothing serious, Alex. We were sent with Bruno to leave cameras and spy devices at the oligarch's home in Monaco."

"So then why didn't we go and say hi to him?"

"I was not sure he would remember me Alex. He was totally drunk."

"Come on, which man can forget you, Angela? Impossible! Listen, I am sorry I asked you all stupid questions . . . I just felt so jealous. Good night, Angela."

"Alex, I want to take it to the next level," Angela said, holding Alex's hand.

Alex felt extremely happy. "Angela, I hoped that one day it would happen and I want to do something . . ."

"What is it, Alex?"

Alex stood on his knee and said: "Angela, I am in love with you and I am yours. Please accept this ring." He took out of his pocket gorgeous Cartier ring.

"Where did you get it?" Angela was amazed.

"I sold the bottle of vodka with the help of producer."

"You sold 100 K euro bottle made of gold to get me ring? Alex, it is the most romantic thing that ever happened in my life."

"So is it yes???" Alex asked, still standing on his knee.

"Yes! Yes! Yes!"

They started kissing passionately.

"Angela, let's open bottle of champagne. It is in the bar." They stepped out onto the terrace, holding glasses with sparkling champagne. The night was young. The night was white. They saw the moon and the sun together. It was such a beautiful moment; they both knew that they will remember it forever. Angela and Alex finished their drinks and came back to the suite. Alex kissed Angela passionately. They hugged each other. Alex started undressing Angela. He almost could not believe it was happening. It felt like a dream. Her skin was so soft. The smell of her perfume was mesmerizing. He just wished this moment would last forever. It was the best night of his life.

*　　*　　*

Finally, on Monday the instructor arrived.

"Sir, the mission is successful," Alex reported.

"I am very happy to hear that. All agents before you guys failed."

"In fact, Sir, not only we managed to place the tracking devices, but we got very interesting proposal to sign contract with Russian producer Dima. I would be happy, Sir, if you could report it cause this offer could be our unique chance to be inside of the oligarch's circle."

"I like the way you think, my boy. But do you realize that in this case yours and Angela's lives will be constantly under threat? We will not be able to rescue you. In case you are caught you will be on your own."

"We discussed it with Angela, Sir, and we are ready to take our chances."

"Very good. I am very happy to hear that both of you are so brave. I will report your proposal. Right now return to your hotel, pack your bags and wait for further instructions."

*   *   *

Tall, handsome man in his late 50ies was sitting on Armani sofa; the sheikh entered the room.

"Any news on oligarch?" the sheikh asked.

The man smiled, "Finally, luck is on our side. We got a chance to make our guys part of the oligarch's inner circle, your highness."

The sheikh laughed, "That's great news, *sadig!*–friend! We should celebrate tonight!"

Hundreds of beautiful belly dancers were shaking their hips, the voice of Arabic singer, repeating *"habibi ya habibi"*, charmed the audience; the smells of delicious kebabs were in the air. Ministers, businessmen, diplomats all came for the sheikh's party. He was in a great mood that night.

*   *   *

Early Tuesday morning the envelope arrived. The letter had only three words, "You can start." Alex and Angela were extremely happy. They finally got their freedom. Though it was not a complete freedom, but relative one—still it was a huge achievement for them.

Alex called the producer, "Dima, I am ready to start." The producer was super excited as he was just about to raise the offer for Alex to 1.5 million euro.

"Alex, my boy, please get ready. Tomorrow we are going to choose a song."

Choosing the song seemed to be such a hard task. They read so much crap. It was next to impossible to get the lyrics right.

After reading 200 songs, Alex said, "Dima, give me a few days and I will write some lyrics for the song."

The producer agreed to Alex's suggestion, "OK, my boy, you try."

After 4 days Alex came with this song:

I see you in the moonlight you are so beautiful!

I see you in the daylight you are so beautiful!

You are so beautiful, beautiful, beautiful!

I see you in the moonlight.

I see you in the daylight.

You . . . I love you! You . . . I love you!

"I don't know, Alex, it sounds good but . . . ." producer said.

"Dima, please no 'but'. Just trust me on that!"

"My boy, the music video will cost us around 200 K euro, let's better go with famous lyricist. This sounds too simple . . ."

"Sir, let's do like that: first we record the song, then we put it on YouTube and you see the reaction."

The recording took 5 more days, and then they uploaded the song on YouTube.

The song passed three million hits in first day itself.

"My boy, we start shooting our video next Monday," producer said.

*   *   *

Angela got her costume, "What is it?" she asked the designer.

"Well," the gay designer said, "my vision is at night you turn into sexy hot creature . . . so you will be wearing these black G-string panties. You will be topless except for these black roses on your chest."

Alex entered the room, the designer Mudashkin shouted, "Oh, look at our star, he is so handsome. I want to hug him!" Alex kept safe distance. Mudashkin sent blowing kisses. "How is my creation, Alex? Angela will wear these black G-string panties and black roses. It will be real black magic, huh?" Alex saw Angela was about to punch the poor designer.

"My friend, my greatest designer Mudashkin, it is very creative . . . but we need to do slight changes . . ."

"OK," Mudashkin sounded slightly sad.

"See the roses are very nice idea but we need to make them white and put on her head not chest."

"OK, Alex" the designer was almost crying.

"The G-string is good idea but we make panties nude color and put them under a dress . . . The dress will be the most beautiful that you have ever created . . . I think it will be golden color long dress,"

Alex closed his eyes for a second. He opened his eyes and said, "Yes, golden dress with Swarovski crystals. It will be out of this world . . . This dress will be everywhere: on the covers of magazines, TV, Internet. All the girls in Russia will want dress like this! Your sales will be huge after this video becomes super hit!"

"I like it, Alex!" the designer Mudashkin shouted.

"My friend, you are so creative! You are such a great designer. I am so happy with you!" Alex continued, "Your idea of golden dress is perfect!"

Mudashkin hugged Alex, "Oh! I love you, my sweet boy. OK, I have to run now. I want to create my golden goddess dress. If I design it fast, I can use the dress for Fashion Week. Bye!" Mudashkin left.

"I underestimated you, Alex," Angela said, "How did you manage to convince him? He never changes designs for anyone!"

"I think I deserve a kiss," Alex smiled.

"Yes, sweetheart," Angela gave him long passionate kiss.

The song shooting was going really well, Angela's dress was elegant. She looked like a dream. Alex was checking her shots on monitor. The result was great. Producer Dima was extremely happy. The new boy turned into gold anything he touched. Hardly one month in St. Petersburg, the boy got a perfume ad. The only thing that worried the producer that the boy wanted to promote his girl everywhere. She was gorgeous . . . but even when Alex got a perfume ad offer, he refused to sign a contract without Angela. Now their hoardings were all over the country. Dima needs to explain to the boy, that for Alex's career it is better to be alone or with several girls, but not with the same girl all the time.

*   *   *

Alex kept hacking in his limo. He managed to get lots of information, but it seemed next to impossible to get new secure line for Mike . . . Suddenly, he noticed new folders; they were saved as hidden by administrator, so he almost missed them. He started downloading video: it was Angela. Alex did not even know why he kept watching it. Professors asked her to be nice to new guy–that was him. His heartbeat fastened: next video. He could not believe it . . . Angela was chosen as the perfect virgin for his profile! They use her to make him a murderer. Time stopped for him. He could hardly breathe. He was betrayed. She never loved him. He felt all his dreams were broken . . .

His device finally hacked the system. He got secure line for Mike. Angela opened the door, smiling.

"Hey, sweetheart, you are working too hard, get some rest, darling." He looked at Angela as if he saw her for the first time: "What an actress!" He would never guess that she never loved him, that it was all game . . . He was just being played.

"Did you manage to get secure line for Mike?"

"Yes, I did. Here!"

"Hey, my love, what's wrong, you seem to be upset?" Angela asked.

"Upset?" Alex felt so angry he could hardly control himself and not shout: "Upset??? You lied to me . . . They told you to become my friend!"

Angela seemed to be surprised for a second. It felt like she remembered the meeting. "Oh . . . that was long time ago. You just came to the castle: so they wanted me to help you to get integrated into the school community."

"OK," Alex said, "and what about the seduction? That was also part of the plan?"

"What are you talking about, Alex?"

"Angela, enough is enough! I am not going to believe any of your new lies!"

"Listen Alex . . ."

Alex grabbed his bag and said, "Angela, it's over! Don't try to contact me ever again!" Angela was totally shocked. She opened Alex's computer; when she saw the video she felt disgusted, "How dare they play with people's emotions? Who do they think they are? Gods?"

CHAPTER 9

CAN YOU SEE THE FUTURE?

Cheng as always came first to *krav maga* class. He was the best in all types of martial arts in the school. He started meditating. He remembered what he read about ancient masters. No matter how fast, strong or what sophisticated technique their opponent would have, the ancient master could still defeat his enemy. How? He would simply predict the movement. The moment the person starts fighting, he will have a thought. All you need to do is to catch his thought first and then defeat him. Most of students thought it is nonsense. Cheng's heart told him it was true.

"OK, students," the Master entered the classroom. All kinds of rumors surrounded him in the castle: that he was brought up by ninjas and later became an FBI agent; that he once defeated 30 world's best fighters at an illegal competition. "Today, we continue with *krav maga*. It is a form of Israeli street combat, used by soldiers. *Krav maga* is very real, very fast. The only rule is there is no rule. You either kill or get killed." The

Master showed the first moves. "OK, now everybody should take a partner and start practicing." They all got busy polishing the moves. "OK," the Master shouted, "Now, we are going to do mini championship." Cheng's first opponent was Adams, very fast and strong fighter. Cheng tried to get back to that special state of mind: "Don't think; just feel what your partner is going to do next." Suddenly, Cheng got it. It was overwhelming . . . he felt exactly what Adams would do next.

"Cheng is the winner," the Master announced.

The opponents kept changing; Cheng was paired against Raj, Mike, Benny, Sam, and he managed to beat them all. It was just perfect. "OK," the Master shouted, "The lesson is over. Our champion is Cheng." Cheng left the class. "It was true!" Cheng thought, walking back to his room, "Ancient masters did not lie. It existed."

CHAPTER 10

YOU EITHER KILL OR GET KILLED IN SINGAPORE

On Tuesday the helicopter came for them. "Cheng and Aimee, get ready you are going to Singapore," the instructor said. Cheng was super excited it was his first journey to Asia.

In the evening of arrival Aimee persuaded Cheng to go to Marina Bay casino, the queue was very long. Indians, Indonesians, Pilipino, Australians, and British–all these foreigners came to try their luck.

They both showed passports to the security. "Please sir, please madam," the Singaporean guy welcomed. They entered the casino–it was huge–very modern with machines for all kind of tastes.

Aimee suggested, "Hey, Cheng, let's try our luck. I have five hundred bucks. Let's play a roulette". Cheng looked at Aimee again: she was stunning–tall, fair, black curly hair and amazing blue eyes. Cheng and Aimee came to low level roulette tables.

"OK, so 6 black?" Aimee asked. Suddenly, Cheng got the same feeling like during the *krav maga* mini championship. It was incredible. He knew which number was going to win.

"Listen, put 500 on 1."

"Are you sure, Cheng?"

"Yes, Aimee, maximum I will give you money back."

"OK, cool."

"No more stakes!" The ball kept rolling, it started slowing down. "1 red wins!" the dealer shouted. Aimee could not believe it. She kissed Cheng.

"17 500 Singaporean dollars. It is huge, Cheng! I can't believe it, we just won."

"Aimee, you won . . ."

"Come on, Cheng. Half is yours. You told me the number."

"Are you playing?" the croupier asked.

"No," Aimee answered, "we are cashing out and going to the bar to celebrate." She left a 100 Singaporean dollar tip for the dealer.

The drinks finally got over and they went up to the room. Aimee was really high; she started kissing Cheng passionately in the lift. Cheng could hardly control himself. They reached the room. He opened the door. Aimee whispered to his ear, "Come and have me on this big bed". Cheng knew that if he did this now, he would regret later. After all, Aimee was drunk; he could not take advantage of her. He brought a bottle of water and a tablet of aspirin for her.

"Aimee, please have it."

"I am not drunk," Aimee protested, "I can still stand straight". She tried walking in her high heel stiletto sandals, but fell down on the bed. He covered her with blanket. She fell asleep really fast. Cheng went to take a shower. He remembered passionate kisses of Aimee in the lift. It was amazing: real French kiss from really hot French girl.

*   *   *

The instructor got a call: Aimee and Cheng got caught on camera. They are exposed.

Next morning the instructor came in their room. "Well, I have bad news for you guys. You are exposed."

"That is impossible! We followed the procedure completely."

"I don't know guys. I am just here to do what I was told to. Here are new passports, you need to go to Canada and stay there. I have 10 K euro for you here."

"How can we contact you, Sir?"

"No, Cheng, you can't. We will contact you in a week." The instructor avoided looking into their eyes.

"What do you mean?" Aimee cried, "You can't just leave us like that. In the school they always say that we are family, we will always protect each other."

"I am sorry, guys, I need to leave now, do not try to follow me or get back into school on your own. We will contact you when the time is right." Instructor closed the door.

"They used us!" Aimee shouted, "What are we going to do now? We are exposed so they moved on us. They threw us like used garbage bags." Cheng kept silence.

"Cheng, say something."

"Aimee, we need to check out immediately. If we are exposed the other guys can try to kill us." They checked out and moved to Ritz.

"Why Ritz, Cheng?"

"Cause it is safe and most probably they will expect us to be at airport, but we will stay here. Let's go to the Universal studio."

"Are you mad, Cheng? We can get killed any moment and all what you are thinking about is to click a picture with Marylin Monro?"

"Actually that is nice idea, Aimee, but I was thinking we should try our luck in a casino."

"Oh," Aimee laughed, "OK, let's go." They got a cab. The Universal studio was great fun. They got an Ancient Egypt ride and then sat in a typical old NY style pizzeria. It felt like time stopped here. Aimee looked like she was enjoying their break.

"Cheng, I am really happy that you are here". She held his hand, "I don't know what I would do without with you?"

Cheng smiled, "Aimee, I don't know how to say that. I am . . . I really feel so close to you . . . I want to protect you. I guess I am falling in love with you."

"I know, Cheng . . . That night in the hotel you could have taken advantage of me, but you didn't! I knew at that time itself you are serious about me . . ."

Cheng felt really happy. "Come on, Aimee, we should try to win."

They went to the roulette table. They stood near it for a few minutes. Cheng could clearly feel which numbers were coming. He put 900 on 1.

A few minutes later the croupier shouted, "1 red wins!"

Aimee and Cheng went to cash it out.

Late in the evening Aimee and Cheng were back to hotel.

"OK, Aimee, so we got enough money. We should stay here till Thursday, but from now on we can't go out of the hotel.

On Thursday morning Cheng said, "I think we should do check in and security check separately, we will meet in the plane."

"I am scared, Cheng!" Aimee answered.

"Don't be scared, Aimee, it will be all fine. We got business class. Less people mean fewer chances to get killed." Immigration and security check went well.

Finally, Aimee and Cheng got on the plane. They didn't take any food or drinks in case somebody would try to poison them. Soon the crew switched off lights to give some rest for the passengers.

Cheng went to the toilet just to check out if he is being followed. Immediately, one guy went after him like a shadow. It was quite dark, but Cheng could still see the syringe in a stranger's hand. Without hesitation, he grabbed the enemy's hand and injected the guy. Before losing consciousness the man managed to whisper to Cheng, "You can't escape, boy! There are others . . . they are coming after you."

Cheng put the guy on the chair and covered him with blanket. Aimee didn't see anything. She fell asleep. Before landing the airhostess came to the stranger's chair and said, "Excuse me, Sir, you need to put your chair into the landing position." She touched the man. He fell down on the floor. The airhostess started screaming. The guy was dead. Cheng knew it could be Aimee or him instead of the guy. Aimee looked scared. At the airport Cheng said, "We have to stay here, we can't take the transit flight and we need to change our clothes." They stopped in Zurich.

CHAPTER 11

HOT RUSSIAN BABES

Alex came to the recording studio in a very bad mood. Everybody felt it. The fat producer entered the studio.

"Hey, my star, how are you? What's wrong?"

"Nothing," Alex said.

"Come on, my golden boy, you can tell me everything. I am like your mother, father, best friend and nanny. I have to nurture the talent."

"We fought . . ."

"Angela and you?"

"Yes . . . But I don't want to talk about it," Alex answered.

"Relax, my boy, in St. Petersburg there are more beautiful girls than waves in Baltic Sea. One is gone the other is coming. Let's take a day off."

"Driver," the fat producer called, "take us to *banya*–Russian sauna."

"Alex, my superstar, in Russia the best place to relax and have a drink during the day is at *banya*."

Producer SMSed Masha, "Alex fought with Angela. We are going to sauna."

Masha got SMS. "Wow, Dasha, the hottest guy in Russia is single again! Let's catch him before others!"

Alex and producer entered the *banya*. They got masseuses: the girls were semi naked. "Please, Alex, autograph," one of them whispered in sexy voice, "I am such a big fan of yours."

The producer said, "Girls, first you finish this massage."

The table had it all: vodka, pickled cucumbers, caviar, black bread, butter.

"Come on, my superstar, have one drink! You will feel better." Alex lost count of his drinks. Suddenly, security guy opened the door, Masha and Dasha entered. To call their costumes bikini would be same as to call tiny belt a skirt. There was nothing left to imagination. Alex was already drunk and he looked at them longer than would be decent, but the girls felt that Alex was finally impressed by their hot bodies.

"Hi, Alex, you remember us we were with Vlad at the club—we are Dasha and Masha?"

The producer was happy: Alex liked the girls.

"Yes, I remember you, girls," Alex answered.

"They are so hot!" the producer interrupted.

"Yes, they are . . . impressive!" Alex kept looking at Masha's boobs. They looked enormous!

Masha moved the chair closer to Alex, "Alex, sweetheart, you seem to be tensed I have to give you massage." Before he could refuse Masha put her huge boobs, hardly covered by bikini top, on Alex's naked torso.

"What kind of massage is it?" Alex shouted.

Masha smiled sweetly, "This the best massage: big boobies massage!"

"Come on, Masha, stop it we have already booked professional masseuses," Alex said. Masha stopped, but she looked unhappy.

"I can do even better!" Dasha jumped from her chair and started doing lap dance. Afterwards, she moved closer to Alex and rubbed her booty against his body: slowly and seductively. Alex felt really uncomfortable. He gently moved Dasha away.

Dasha looked disappointed, "Why are you resisting yourself, Alex? I know you want me . . . I could feel you."

"Listen, Dasha, you are very pretty girl, but I am not ready for a new relationship."

"So let's just have fun!" Dasha laughed, "Let's jump into the pool."

Alex and producer followed Masha and Dasha. The girls removed their bikinis and started teasing Alex. Alex kept safe distance from the hot Russian babes and continued drinking vodka with Dima.

"Don't splash water on us, girls, it may come into our drinks!" the producer shouted.

"Come on, Dima, we are better than vodka! Enjoy with us, forget drinks!"

Alex called the waiter, "Please organize towels for the girls."

"Yes, Sir, actually, my girlfriend is a big fan of yours; can I take photo with you, please?"

"Later, not now!" the producer interrupted. Dima didn't notice that the waiter had already clicked photos of Alex with Masha and Dasha.

"So, my superstar, do you still think about Angela?" the producer asked.

"Just don't mention her name any more," Alex answered.

CHAPTER 12

RISKY BUSINESS

The handsome man admired huge diamond on his finger. He picked up the phone, "Sir, I have some bad news. The boy and the girl escaped, Sir. Our man is dead. They did not reach Canada," Ahmed reported.

"Idiots! You can't do anything right!" shouted the rich man and disconnected.

*   *   *

"Aimee," Cheng said, "If we want to live we need to be smarter than them . . . We can't go to a hotel again. Let's rent a villa near Zurich."

They managed to get the villa without any problem. Three weeks passed.

"Cheng, we can't hide like that forever in Switzerland. One day they will catch us and kill."

"We need a help, Aimee."

"Whom should we ask, Cheng?"

"I got good feeling about Alex."

"Are you sure, Cheng?"

"Yes. I know it is huge risk . . . but you are right, Aimee, staying here is also not an option." He finally managed to hack into MTS system to get Alex's number

*   *   *

Alex was standing on the terrace. The headache was back . . . without Angela in his life he did not see any the reason to continue: his life was purposeless again. Angela was just a dream. She was never real. She never loved him. She just did what she was told by professors. He moved one step closer. Alex could almost see himself fly . . . and then die. "Will she at least feel sad for a moment?" Alex wondered. Suddenly, his phone rang.

"Hey, Alex, it is Cheng. I am in bad situation. The school left me and some guys are trying to kill me and Aimee." Alex could not believe what he just heard.

"Alex . . . are you there?"

"Yes, Cheng," Alex stepped back from the terrace.

"I know it sounds mad, but can you help me?"

Alex laughed, "You know what Cheng you just saved my life . . . I was about to commit suicide. I will help you."

Cheng smiled. It seems after all there was a hope.

Alex called producer, "I want to shoot my new clip in Zurich."

"That's the spirit my boy."

*   *   *

Two burqa ladies, accompanied by man, entered the suite in Zurich. Alex was alone. The guy stayed in the hall. The ladies entered the main room. They removed the burqas.

"Hey, my friends, I can't believe you are here," Alex said.

"I am so happy you decided to help us, Alex."

"No problem, Cheng. Tell me what happened?" Cheng told him the whole story.

"That's crazy," Alex just kept saying, "I thought we could trust the school."

"Where is Angela?" Cheng asked.

"We fought . . ."

"I can't believe it, Alex, you guys were so much in love! Angela always tried to protect you from us. You we not really Mr. Popular in the castle, you know it," Cheng interrupted.

"I hacked the system and found videos: Angela was just following instructions. First, to be my friend and then . . . to seduce me."

"It can't be true, before you Angela never looked at any guy like she did at you," Aimee added.

"No way, Aimee, she was just doing what they told her to!" Alex argued.

"They could have told her something . . . but her feelings were real!" Aimee concluded.

"OK, leave all this guys, I got you all proper papers you can come with me now as my crew."

"You know what, Alex," Cheng smiled, "I think we should not run and hide anymore."

"OK, so what you want to do, guys?"

"Can we sing . . . in your video, Alex?"

"In my clip?" Alex asked.

"Yes, Alex, I will sing in Chinese. Aimee will sing in French and you can make publicity that you are already star in Russia and now you decided to win hearts in France and China 'cause Russian, French and Chinese people have great love and respect for each other."

"Seems like I need to hire you as my new PR agent," Alex joked, "but what will it give you, guys? Any killer will be able to find you fast as you will become famous."

"Exactly, Alex, but you see if we get killed after the release of video, the murder will draw a lot of attention: they will be scared to kill us!"

"Cheng, you know what . . ." Alex said after long pause, "I think you are right."

"OK, then let's do that," Cheng smiled.

"I just hope guys . . . you actually can sing."

Alex called the music director. "What! Now? Alex, it is impossible: I can't do it! Oh, you are ready to pay so much! OK, I will be there tomorrow."

*   *   *

The handsome man was having massage at Burj Khalifa suite in Dubai.

"Ahmed, any news on the Chinese guy and that French girl?"

"No, Sir. Maybe, they were killed."

The man changed the TV channel. "What's the f.ck? This is that b.stard why is he on TV and not in the grave yard? Ahmed, get me secure line immediately!"

"Yes, Sir."

"Have you seen this Chinese guy and French babe on TV? What's happening? What games are you playing with me? You promised me they would be both dead."

*　　*　　*

Alex's phone rang.

"Alex, how are you?" Professor Goldman asked.

"I am good, Sir."

"In your last clip you put Cheng and Aimee."

"Yes, Sir, just like you ordered me to make them stars as soon as possible, using all my contacts in show business."

"Oh," after long pause Professor Goldman said, "OK, Alex, when did you get this order?"

"Last month through your instructor like usual, Sir . . . Anything else, Sir?"

"No, just arrange secure phone line for Cheng. I will contact him in a few days."

"Yes, Sir."

"OK, my boy, you are doing great job."

"Thank you, Sir."

Cheng was sitting almost pale.

"Did it work?" he asked.

"I think so," Alex replied.

"Hopefully, Alex, it will! We are on the edge . . ."

*　　*　　*

Ahmed passed the phone to the handsome man in Prada.

"What now?" the man sounded frustrated. "I can't believe it, such a young boy, but so brilliant. He fooled everyone! Yes, Professor Goldman, you are right, we can't kill him now. He became overnight hit in China. My assistants got me all info. Just check out what is on this b.stard's mind. What he wants?" The man disconnected.

*   *   *

Cheng got a call in three days.
"Cheng, it is Professor Goldman."
"Yes, Sir."
"Cheng, why did you lie to Alex?"
"I had no any other option, Sir. I could not tell Alex about operation because this information was top secret and I did not know how else to contact you, Sir. The instructor told us to wait for one week. We waited for two weeks, but nobody contacted us . . . I persuaded Aimee to follow me."
"OK, I see . . . ell, you took very dangerous step, my boy."
"I am sorry, Sir."
"I think it was smart decision, my boy . . . Now we can send you to China."
"Thank you, Sir."
"Bye, my boy."

*   *   *

"What do you think, Professor Goldman, is Cheng dangerous?"

"No, he is just a small stupid boy. He is like a puppy . . . left without master and trying to find him back."

"So we let him live?" the handsome man in Burj Khalifa suite asked.

"Yes, him and the girl," Professor Goldman answered.

CHAPTER 13

VLADIMIR—THE OLIGARH

Angela was heartbroken and distressed. She tried to get some sleep, but she couldn't. She stepped out onto the terrace to get some fresh air. She did so much to escape her prison . . . that's what the castle meant for her, but now she was in so much pain that she would prefer staying in that prison than feeling this. She went back to the room, she noticed a bottle of vodka, "OK, just one drink to feel better," Angela decided.

*   *   *

One week after Alex broke up with Angela, his manager called the producer, "What to do about the bills of Angela's suite? Alex moved out."

"Let the girl pay . . . if she doesn't, tell her to move out. Alex doesn't care anymore for her! He moved on," Dima answered.

*　　*　　*

Angela woke up, her head was paining. She came to the door and saw newspaper. It was Alex with those vulgar babes. "The Superstar Alex moved on! Two Hot Babes is better that one sweet Angel . . . ah?" the headline said.

Angela felt betrayed: "How could he forget her so fast?" Her hand went for a drink. The pain was too much too handle. She started crying.

*　　*　　*

Vlad the oligarch called the producer: "Is it true . . . about Alex?"

"Yes, Vlad! Alex moved on. He almost f..d Dasha in front of me."

"OK, Dima, where is Angela now?"

"I think she is still in the Europe hotel, but I told my manager either make her pay the bills or get her out of the suite . . . 'cause Alex is not going to pay for her !"

"Dima you know, Alex is just a small boy; he can't treat the poor girl like that. She is not a toy. Today he plays with her, tomorrow throws away. He doesn't deserve her, I will pay the bills."

"I agree, Vlad. I am sorry I wanted to throw her out. I didn't know you liked the girl. You know, Vlad, I am just producer of Alex, but you are my best friend."

"Don't worry, Dima. I am not angry with you."

"Thanks, Vlad."

*　　*　　*

Vlad, the oligarch, had huge bouquet of flowers, he rang the bell.

"It's him," Angela thought, "Alex is back! It can't be hotel stuff cause I put do not disturb sign." She felt so happy. All she saw was huge bouquet of flowers.

"Alex," Angela shouted, "You are back my love!"

Vlad entered the door, "No it is not Alex. It's me."

Angela could hardly control her tears.

"Kitten, you look bad . . . how much did you drink?" Vlad asked.

"I don't know, Vlad, please leave me alone."

"Angela, you know drinking will make the pain just worse. Come on, sweetie, you need to get out of here."

"No, Vlad, just leave me!" Angela shouted.

"Listen, kitten, you will get drunk later, but now go to take a shower!"

"I just want to be alone, Vlad!" Angela cried.

Vlad grabbed Angela and took her to the bathroom and put her into a cold shower.

"What's wrong with you, Vlad?" Angela shouted, "Are you mad, Vlad?"

"Angela, I am sorry, but you need to move on! I give you 10 minutes to get dressed, if you don't–I will take you with me in your bathrobe. It will be embarrassing . . ."

Vlad called his assistant: "Pay the bill and book the appointment at beauty salon at 8.30 pm."

In 10 minutes Angela was dressed.

"Are you happy now, Vlad?"

"No, babe, not yet!"

"Where are you taking me to?"

"To beauty salon."

"What nonsense, Vlad!"

"You . . . smell babe!"

"I don't . . ."

"You do, babe."

Angela felt embarrassed. She realized, she did not wash her hair for a long time.

They entered the salon.

"Girls, she should look her best, if I am happy everybody gets a 100 euro tip. She is all yours," Vlad said.

Angela felt humiliated: these girls were reading about Alex and Russian singers.

"Sweetie, I am sorry," the hairstylist said and started washing Angela's hair.

Angela felt like crying again.

"Don't cry, sweetie," the hair stylist advised, "You should look your best and make the bast . . . d understand what he has lost!"

The make-up girl added: "Yes, Angela, make the son of the b.tch regret and you know . . . you are too lucky, babe."

"Lucky?" Angela asked.

"I mean, babe, you are with Vlad," the make-up girl continued.

"We are just friends."

"Don't be stupid, Angela. Girls are dying to be with Vlad. Vlad is a real man! I know Vlad likes you. Well, the way he looks at you. I wish I could go out with a guy like Vlad. I mean Alex is handsome, but he has no substance. Vlad is handsome, hot and he is a real man! Vlad has money to buy thousand stars like Alex. Nobody can buy Vlad. Vlad is a big league, babe!"

The hairstylist washed her hair, put a leave-on conditioner and then started the blow dry. Angela's hair looked great now.

"Babe!" the stylist smiled, "Now you look hot again."

Angela's make-up was on the edge: smokey eyes and red hot lips. It was almost like saying, "Hey, I am ready for the battle. I want to win hearts again."

Vlad was waiting on the couch. "Girls, amazing job! You know what you deserve 200 euro each."

"So sweet of you, Vlad," the make-up girl said, "When are you taking me out for a date, Vlad?" Vlad smiled.

"OK, Angela, we need to leave now," Vlad said, looking at his Swiss limited edition watch.

"You are so lucky, Angela! I wish I were you," the make-up girl shouted.

"Vlad, girls love you," Angela said.

"I am a regular client: good tips, no bad attitude," Vlad explained.

"They say you are a real man, Vlad."

"And you? What do you think, Angela? You want to find out?" Vlad asked.

There was so much sexual energy in his eyes that Angela felt shy and looked down.

"Now we should get you a dress, Angela," Vlad continued.

"But I have enough of clothes," Angela protested.

"No more old stuff! You start your life from a new page, Angela."

Suddenly, Angela noticed she still wore the ring that Alex had given her. She said to the billionaire, "Vlad, I need to speak with the concierge."

"OK, Angela, I will wait for you right here," he sat down on the sofa.

Angela walked over to the reception desk, took an empty envelope from the concierge and placed the ring inside. She wondered for a second, should she leave a message? Just then, Angela happened to glance at a large photo of Alex with those vulgar Russian singers on the front page of the newspaper, lying on the desk.

She handed the envelope to concierge, "Please give to Alex–the superstar!" she said, pointing out at the newspaper.

The concierge gave her an understanding look, "Certainly, Miss, anything else I can do for you?"

"No, that's all," replied Angela to him. "Hopefully Alex is happy now," she thought.

Turning away, she walked towards Vlad, who was waiting for her on the sofa.

"Baby, let's go shopping," the oligarch said, "The shop is in the same building, we need to turn left now."

Angela and Vlad entered the famous Babochka shop at the Europe hotel.

"Vlad, welcome back!" the shop assistant said in sweet gay voice, "We just got new Armani suits. Would you like to try?"

"No, thanks, Valera, tonight I want to choose something amazing for the lady."

"Alright, Vlad your wish is my command. Miss, please come with me down stairs. We have great selection."

Angela followed the shop assistant. "You are so lucky! Vlad can change your future in a second. He is super rich . . . super generous. Girl, you hit jackpot! Sorry I talk too much," the shop assistant said.

Angela smiled and answered, "I think you are right. He is great guy."

"Great is not the right word, Angela. I asked once Vlad to give me a loan for my brother's college . . . Vlad just paid the whole amount and refused to take any money back. He is amazing guy, Angela!"

"OK, Angela, I got this Dior dress yesterday from Paris, just try it, the changing room is there. *Magnifique*! So beautiful!" the shop assistant admired. "Vlad will love this dress!"

Angela went upstairs. Vlad whistled when he saw her, "Babe, you are hot! This red dress . . . Wow!"

Vlad gave a 100 euro tip to the shop assistant, "Thanks, Valera, great choice—as always."

"OK, let's go, babe," Vlad said. The driver opened the limo door for Angela. She started feeling happy again.

"Where are you taking me, Vlad?"

"I am kidnapping the most beautiful girl in the world so that only I could see her."

"Come on, Vlad, tell me."

"Well, kitten, your look is not complete." They stopped near the Cartier shop.

"Cartier?" Angela asked.

"Yes, kitten. You deserve the best!"

They entered the shop.

"Welcome back, Sir," the manager greeted Vlad.

"Hey, how are you doing?" Vlad asked.

"I am doing well and even better now after seeing you, Sir. What would you be interested in today, Sir?"

"Show us your best necklace," Vlad asked.

"Please Sir, Madam, have a seat. Would you like a cup of coffee, tea?"

"No, thanks."

The assistants ran to get their best jewelry. "Please, Sir, Madam, these are my 5 best pieces."

"I like this one," Vlad said.

"Sir, you have a great taste! This one is my favorite piece," manager told Vlad.

"What do you think, Angela?"

"It is the best," Angela confirmed.

"Also I want the girl's name on this certificate."

Angela interrupted, "Vlad, I am sorry, I can't accept this."

"Angela it is a gift, I told you already in Monaco. I don't take gifts back," Vlad explained.

"I love this necklace, Vlad. OK, then I will pay you back," she said and then realized all money that she had earned went into Alex's account. He never gave her money, she had nothing.

"Thanks, Vlad."

Vlad smiled, "I just want you to feel happy."

Angela understood Vlad didn't want her to go through humiliation; he wanted her to feel safe and not to ask money from anyone. Vlad knew she would never accept cash as it would make her feel cheap, so he offered her this stunning necklace. It was all because of Alex, he left her in such a miserable position.

"You are a real man, Vlad," Angela said.

"Well, Angela, after such a big compliment I have to take you to a party," Vlad joked.

They entered the most happening club in St. Petersburg and went to the VIP-zone. Most of Vlad's friends were surprised. The billionaire came with one girl. It was a clear message. He never did that before.

"Hey, Vlad," the supermodel Natasha smiled, "Let me hug you. You look hot!" Natasha looked at Angela and said, "Hello An . . . Angela, right? Liked your clip babe."

Angela felt that the waiters were extra polite; everybody: models, actors, designers were giving her attention because she came with Vlad.

Vlad said, "Angela, please meet my dear friend–Max. He is CEO of the most happening ad agency. Max, I heard you wanted new face for the jewelry ad. Angela will be perfect, right?"

"Yes, sure Vlad. She is fantastic."

"OK, Max, thanks."

"Cheers, my friends, for the most beautiful girl in my life; cheers for Angela!"

It was almost 4 am.

"Shall we go to your place to party, Vlad?" supermodels Natasha and Bella asked.

"No, girls, I am going with Angela: only two of us. Bye, guys!"

After they left the party Vlad's friends were still shocked.

"What did he find in her?" supermodel Natasha asked.

"I don't know, babe. It's crazy," supermodel Bella answered.

"I think Vlad is in love with her," Max added.

"I hate this b.tch," Natasha said.

* * *

Vlad and Angela entered Vlad's duplex. Vlad went to take a shower and told Angela: "Babe, you also take a shower, that's the second door on the left. Towels are already there."

Vlad was enjoying his espresso. "I always have a cup of coffee after a party," Vlad explained. Angela removed her towel. She started walking slowly and seductively towards Vlad.

"What is it, kitten?" Vlad looked surprised.

"Vlad, I just need you to love me now."

Vlad started laughing.

"What's wrong with you, Vlad?" Angela felt bad that he laughed at her; she rapped herself in the towel again.

"I don't know, baby, it just seemed awkward. Hey, Angela, look at the camera–Alex is there at the lobby. He is knocking at the door."

"Where?" Angela asked and ran to see the camera. Vlad's eyes looked sad when he watched Angela running to check Alex on camera . . .

When she turned back, Vlad managed to control his emotions.

"That's what I am saying, Angela. Alex was not there, baby. I just wanted to see how fast you will run to get a glimpse of him."

Angela looked down at the floor. She felt ashamed.

Vlad came very close to her, hugged her so tight that she could feel his muscular body under her towel. "Kitten, I want to get into here," he touched her body through towel, "but only when I will be here," he moved his hand near her heart. I don't want to be number two. I need to be the only one. This is your flat now, kitten. That's your new phone; I am number one on your speed dial. That's my assistant's card, he will do whatever you need," Vlad said and left.

"He is a real man!" Angela thought, falling asleep. The next morning Angela's phone kept ringing nonstop. Top designers wanted her to walk ramp for them. She got an offer to become face of famous jewelry company. Vlad's recommendation was like the order for fashion industry. It felt like everybody wanted to work with her now. Days were passing. Vlad used to take her out almost every weekend, but he still didn't cross the line. It almost felt like he wanted Angela to take the first step.

CHAPTER 14

BETRAYAL

Mike could not sleep last night. Bipasha disappeared . . . just like Max, Deepika and so many of his good friends in the castle. Five days passed. Finally, Mike managed to hack security system and SMS Angela.

"How are you, cool dude?"

"Too bad, baby doll."

"Why? What happened?"

"Bips she . . . she disappeared."

"Are you sure?" Sometimes they had classes in a different campus.

"I am sure, baby doll, she disappeared just like Deepika and Max!"

"OK, I got it. Then let's try to hack." It was easier to hack together. Finally, they managed to get through firewall. OK, that's the file of Bipasha. All was classified. Here . . . that's the latest video! Angela was frozen with fear.

On the screen they showed Bips laying in hand and leg cuffs on the bed, somebody put needles in her body. Bips was crying from unbearable pain.

"So, Bipasha, are you sure you can't kill the minister?"

"It is impossible. I prefer to die. I am jain." (Jain is devotee of ancient religion. The follower of Jainism can't hurt any living creature).

"Nurse, remove the needles," the professor ordered. Bipasha was bleeding. "Bring the leeches. Put them here." The blood suckers started enjoying the feast, they loved the taste of Bipasha's blood.

"Bipasha, I am very kind human being. I give you last chance. You still have time to change your mind . . . till you have enough blood. Think fast because blood suckers will finish you soon," the professor said.

"Why are you doing this to me?" Bipasha cried, "I thought you are my family."

"Your mission is to serve the country," the professor answered.

"I love my country, but I am not a murderer. I can't kill."

"Bipasha, you wasted enough of my time. You are small stupid girl totally useless. Nurse, insert a needle. The girl screams too loud."

One more needle entered Bipasha's body. Bips appeared to lose consciousness from pain. It was horrible. Angela couldn't control her tears.

Mike was so angry.

"Baby doll, we have to do something! I will take them down: all this fu..king castle! They are murderers! They lied to us. They said the castle is our home and they are our family. They promised they will protect us."

"Dude, please come down."

"I will expose them. I will send all data to CNN, BBC . . . each and every news channel."

"Dude, you know we are not strong yet. We can't break the code. If you send the data now, they will kill all of us. They will not let anyone alive."

"At least we can try, doll. I can't let it go. Bips died for nothing."

"I don't think she died."

"Why are you saying this, doll?" Mike looked with hope at the monitor.

"They would have deleted her file completely." That thought made Mike so happy.

"Are you sure, doll?"

"I am guessing, dude."

"So what to do now, doll?"

"I really don't think we can do anything. We just have to break their code first." The hope disappeared from Mike's eyes, he looked almost dead.

"I swear! One day I will take the castle down."

* * *

Next morning the professor came to check on Bipasha. "Nurse, please take care of the patient." The nurse removed all needles, cleaned Bipasha's body and put ointment on her wounds. "Drink this," the nurse ordered. The guards took Bipasha back to her room.

Bipasha got message on her tablet.

"That is weird," Bipasha thought, "Who would send me a message?"

"Bipasha, you need to tell them that you are ready to kill the minister". Bipasha was shocked. They were told that nobody except professors could send messages on a student's tablet. They all tried so hard but none of the students could ever hack the school system. How is it possible that somebody could hack it? I must be a trap.

"Who is it?" Bipasha asked.

"I am your friend."

"Listen, whoever you are . . . I am going to report you!"

"Don't, Bips! It's Mike."

"Are you crazy, Mike?" Bipasha was not sure what happened to her last night was it just a test or was it for real? Can she trust Mike? She tried to act normal.

"You know, Mike, that they can throw you out of the castle for hacking without telling them . . . you should inform professors immediately!"

"Bips, it's more serious than you think. I know what they did with you. Please trust me, Bips. I . . . I really care for you. I don't want you to die."

Bips was totally confused. "Whom can she trust: professors or Mike?

"Bips, I am running out of time. Just watch this video."

"What nonsense, Mike!"

"Just watch it, Bips, then you will understand all and turn away from the mirror as it has a hidden camera with built-in recorder."

"What nonsense, Mike! Listen to me, tomorrow I will need to report that you managed to hack!"

"I don't care, Bips, if you report me. I am ready for that . . . in fact I am ready to die for you right now. But I want you to live."

"Mike, you sound crazy!"

"Just watch it, Bips, and tomorrow we will talk. I need to leave now 'cause the tracking system can catch me."

"Oh God, what should I do now?" Bipasha thought, "If professors are still observing me should I report Mike right now?"

After long thinking, she made up her mind. Bipasha turned away from the mirror and opened the video file.

It was Deepika. She was standing in front of professors.

"So, Deepika? What is your decision, my child? Are you ready to kill the minister?" Professor Wells asked.

"No, Sir. I am Jain, I am pure vegetarian. I don't believe even in killing an animal to feed myself. I can't kill any human being," Deepika answered.

"Did you think well, my child?"

"Yes, Sir! That's my final decision. You know, Sir, the school is my only home. I am ready to work so hard. I am ready to sacrifice my life, but I can't kill anybody!"

"OK, Deepika, then we have no choice but to kill you," Professor Goldman interrupted.

"What?" Deepika looked shocked.

"Yes, Deepika. This world is survival of the fittest we don't need weak agents–like you!"

"Sir, is this some kind of joke?" Deepika asked.

"Joke? No way! Deepika, here is the gun. You need to kill a child."

They guards brought small cute girl, hardly 5 years old.

"Why her?" Deepika asked. The small girl was Indian. She hugged Depika and whispered in Hindi,

"*Didi, mujhe bahut dard lagta hei!*–Big sister, I am very scared!"

"Don't worry, *bachi*," Deepika said to the child.

"Sir, what is happening?" Deepika shouted.

"You have to kill the child, Deepika, if you want to save your life," the professor insisted.

"I am not going to do that! Why do you want to kill this child, Sir?"

"Deepika, this child is of no use to us; her intelligence level did not match our expectations."

"But she is a child, Sir, you always told us that school is our family and here everybody will be ready to die to protect each other. I can't understand, Sir. Is it test?"

"Deepika, wake up! It is not a test! It is reality. You have one hour to decide if you want to live or die," Professor Wells said. All Professors left. They came back one hour later.

"So what is your decision, Deepika? Are you going to save your life or should I kill both of you?"

"I will kill this child," Deepika shouted. She took the gun and pointed it at the head of small girl. Girl started crying in Hindi, "*Didi, nahi!*–Big sister, don't!" Deepika shot, but not the girl, aiming instead at Professor Wells.

Professor Wells smiled, "Stupid Deepika, the gun was not loaded with real bullets. Guards, take them! Deepika, you are are of no use to us now. Nurse, sedate the girls. Guards, take them both to the organs lab." Bipasha saw how the nurse entered the room and sedated both of the girls. The guards brought the girls to the lab. In the lab Bipasha recognized many students: some of them she knew really well. Most of the students were unconscious, but one girl, Lisa, was awoken. Bipasha was always amazed by Lisa's beauty; especially her violet eyes were stunning. The camera moved closer and Bipasha saw the girl's eyes were missing. Bipasha was scared. There was no doubt she saw her own future. Bips didn't want to have her organs removed as well. She started crying. First time in her life Bipasha felt so lonely. What she felt was her home . . . was nothing, but the prison! These professors are evil monsters. They told her, she would be safe here. They lied to Bipasha. They just want to create an army of emotionless cold blooded murderers.

Next morning she was waiting anxiously for Mike to contact her. Finally, she got message from him. "Listen, Bips, this time you have to say you are ready to kill: 'cause they are your family and belonging to family is more important for you than being jain."

"But, Mike, what if they don't believe it?"

"They will believe you, Bips, 'cause they want your type of girl. It is a sophisticated computer program. They want a girl with your profile. They know that one day they will find your type of girl who will agree to kill."

"Mike, what if they ask me to kill the baby?"

"Just do it, Bips! The girl will die anyway, but you will be alive."

"Mike, but I can't kill."

"The gun won't be loaded, Bips. They need the child's organs."

"It is crazy, Mike."

"I know, Bips."

*　　*　　*

Professor Goldman entered the room. "So, what about Bipasha? Is she ready to kill the minister?" Professor Goldman asked.

"No," Professor Kaplan answered.

"Colleagues, I have some interesting news. Today Mike came to find out about Bipasha. I think the boy fell in love with her."

"That's great news, Mr. Kaplan!" Professor Jackson smiled. "Now we just need to break Bipasha and then manipulate Mike, using the girl."

*   *   *

Bipasha could hardly sleep. She was really scared. At 9 am sharp guards escorted her to the room. "Stay here," the guards left her alone. Bipasha felt a cold shiver of fear running through her; she recognized the room from video.

"What did you decide, Bipasha?" The old professor entered the room. "What is your decision? Are you ready to kill the minister? This man brought a lot of trouble to his people and deserves to die," Professor Kaplan said.

Bipasha took a long pause and then answered with confidence: "Yes, Sir, I am ready."

Professor Kaplan looked surprised for a moment and then very happy: "Very well, my child? Why did you decide so?"

"You are my family, Sir, and family comes first. If you tell me to kill, I have to do it."

"Very nice, my child. I am so happy with you. But see I can't trust you just like that. I will bring now a gun and will test you."

In half an hour ten professors entered the room. They all looked excited.

"OK, guards, bring him in," Professor Kaplan ordered. The guards brought small Indian boy. The boy was about 6 years old. His big brown eyes looked so innocent. The child ran towards Bipasha and touched her hand as if asking to protect him.

"Bipasha, take this gun," Mr. Kaplan ordered, "You need to kill the boy now." Bipasha looked shocked. "What happened, Bipasha? We are not your family anymore ? Do you still trust us? Do you dare to question our decision on the fate of the boy?"

Bipasha took the gun, looked into the professor's eyes and said: "Sir, I will kill him!" The boy started running away from Bipasha, screaming for help. Bipasha shot the boy. Her hand did not shake even for a second. The boy fell down. The gun was loaded with real bullets. Bipasha felt her world ended!

"Nice job, Bipasha!" all professors gave her standing ovation.

The boy stood up. He wore a bullet proof vest. Bipasha felt so happy. She is not a murderer, after all.

"Very well, Bipasha," Professor Kaplan concluded, "Today you made all of us proud. You did so well. You were born to be a great agent. Get your bags ready. We will send you soon on your first mission."

Next morning Mike came happy to class. In the night he hacked the video, he found out that Bipasha did well last morning.

Now he needs to find a way to go on the assignment together with Bipasha. Mike waited till students left and then asked Professor Goldman. "Sir, Bipasha, didn't come today. Is she feeling fine?"

The old professor smiled, "What happened, my boy? Are you in love?"

"Yes, Sir, I am," Mike answered, feeling shy.

"Alright, my boy, I see you are blushing. Let me see, what I can do for you."

Mr. Goldman went straight to the professor's room and said "Colleagues, the good news is confirmed. Professor Kaplan, you were right. Mike is in love with Bipasha."

"Mr. Goldman, I believe it is a great idea to send Bipasha and Mike together on the assignment," Professor Johnson suggested.

"All right, Mr. Johnson, but we should make sure nothing happens to the boy. His intelligence level is exceptional. Alex, Angela and Mike are our best hackers."

"I know, Mr. Goldman, but we need to take the risk because if we allow Mike to go with Bipasha we will be his heroes. We need this love to become deeper in order to control him better."

"I agree, Mr. Johnson, we have no choice but to send them together," concluded Mr. Goldman.

CHAPTER 15

SEDUCTION

Angela came to Vlad's room She was naked. Her soft skin was wet after she came out of the shower.

"I need you, Vlad," she whispered. Vlad could not resist, he kissed her lips . . . they were fresh and soft.

Vlad stopped kissing her and looked into Angela's stunning eyes. "You look amazing, baby," Vlad said. Angela smiled. He kissed her hand. "I love you, Angela."

"I love you too, Vlad," she whispered.

"Angela, would you like some cocktail?"

"Yes, Mr. Barman, but I am afraid oligarch-turned-barman will charge me too much for a drink?"

"Not really, Miss, just one smile will be enough."

"Selling yourself short, Vlad, what happened?"

"Your beauty made me lose my mind," Vlad answered. They laughed.

Vlad went to the kitchen. He opened a huge bar and started mixing the drinks.

"Here is your glass," Nina said.

"Nina, what are you doing here?" Vlad looked pale.

"I came to see how fast you will forget me!"

"Nina, I . . ."

"No need to say anything, Vlad! You promised to love me till your last breath, but I guess she is hotter . . . more beautiful than me." Suddenly Nina laughed. "You think she loves you, Vlad? No! She still dreams about her boyfriend–Alex! You are just a fling for her. You betrayed me for nothing!" Nina disappeared. Vlad woke up in cold sweat. It was horrible feeling. He felt bad. He knew Nina died long time ago, but he felt that he is in fact betraying Nina by falling in love with Angela.

CHAPTER 16

THE MINISTER MUST DIE

"Driver, slow down," the minister ordered.

"I don't think so," the driver answered.

"How dare you! Slow down the car right now!" the minister was frustrated. "Hey, security, tell the driver to slow down."

"Sir, you are kidnapped," the security guard answered.

"What?" Minister was angry. "Where is my security guy?" the minister shouted. "You, idiots, you will regret it. Do you know who I am? Immediately stop the car and I will show you mercy."

"Sir, we have the order to kill you," Mike explained.

"To kill me?"

"Sir, we have no time to waste: if you transfer twenty millions dollars into our account we guarantee you will live," Bips answered.

"I don't have twenty million dollars. I am government servant with modest salary."

"Sir, we have no time. Your account number in offshore zone is 609016 . . . 23," Bips said.

"How did you know?" the minister mumbled.

Bipasha told minister: "Sir, please enter your password and finger print here." After the money transfer was over, Bipasha took syringe out of the case.

"No!" the frightened man protested, "You promised to save my life if I give you money."

Bipasha injected minister with unknown drug. The car entered the tunnel.

"Now, we should stop," Bipasha said.

The car stopped exactly over a manhole. Bipasha pulled away carpet and the fake floor of limo, revealing the hole cut into the car.

"Let's remove the manhole cover. Bips, pass me the laser cutter."

"Hurry up, Mike."

"Yes, Bips, working on it!"

"Done, Bips." Mike moved the cover aside and they jumped down into an open manhole. They took minister's body with them. They heard cars honking and moved fast towards the manhole's exit.

"Mike did you see it?"

"That's our boat, Bips."

"We are running out of time, Mike," Bipasha shouted. They jumped onto the boat and Mike grabbed the wheel. "Now, Bips!" yelled Mike, looking at his watch. Bipasha pressed the button and the minister's car bomb exploded. "Bips, finally we are free." Mike kissed Bipasha passionately. They had to move fast.

The plastic surgeon was already waiting for them. They had an appointment fixed. The surgeon did not ask any questions. The minister's face looked extremely ugly. Bipasha and Mike had to put acid on the minister's face to avoid any problems.

"So sad I have to operate such a beautiful girl! Your face is amazing," complained the surgeon, "Anyway, how you want to look?"

"Well, like Merylin Monro?" Bipasha laughed happily. "It doesn't really matter to me."

"OK, and you young man? What you want to look like?"

"Well, I expect to look better than Brad Pit and Robert Pattison. I hope both of them will be fired from Hollywood once their producers will see my new look."

"You guys have great sense of humor, I must say. OK, don't worry you are in good hands. I will do my best," the doctor promised. "Now, guys, jokes apart . . . You want to change your race?" the plastic surgeon continued.

"Well," Bipasha said, "I guess I would not mind a hot Latina look."

"OK, great choice."

"And what about you young man?"

"I don't really know . . . maybe Arabic look?"

"OK, guys. That's possible. Now get some rest, I will start tomorrow."

The surgeries went really well Bipasha and Mike looked totally different. Nobody would be able to recognize them.

"Bips, now we need to get the diction teacher. We must speak in a different accent."

The minister felt miserable, though he looked much better now. He got a face lift and a liposuction for free as a package deal. "So you say it is not safe for me to go home?" the minister asked again.

"Not now, Sir. They still can kill you anytime. These people are so powerful. If you go to your family now they will kill you." The minister looked totally depressed.

"So, kids, why you robbed me off my money?"

"Illegal money that you stole from your people, Sir. Plus, you still have ninety million dollars in your other accounts."

"Whatever," the minister mumbled.

"Sir, we needed money to fight back. We will destroy the agent's school."

"You? You are nothing in front serious guys. You are just kids." Minister was totally depressed. "Oh, God, why did this happen to me?"

"Come on, Sir, cheer up we saved your life," Bipasha said.

"And what life do I have now? I can't do anything here . . . I am a prisoner. My family thinks I am dead. You ruined my life."

"Mike," Bipasha said. "Minister becomes really annoying. What should we do?"

"We have to keep him here till it is all over. I am afraid, Bips, that's the only option. We have no choice."

"I don't know Mike. It feels really bad. Minister is right. It is not life. It is prison. We are not free."

"So what you suggest, Bips?"

"I know it sounds crazy, Mike, but I think we need to fight back right now. We need to finish the agent's school . . . I mean things they did with Deepika."

"It is a great risk, Bips."

"I know, Mike, and it is the just two of us against thousands of them . . ."

"Actually, Bips, I have to tell you something," Mike interrupted, "Angela is also against them."

"Angela? The cute blond Barbie doll? No way!"

"She is, Bips. We should contact her. In fact Angela and I were trying to break the school system code for quite long time."

"Long time?" suddenly jealousy was written all over Bipasha's face.

"Come on, baby, she is not my type."

"Angela is very beautiful girl," Bipasha argued.

"Bips, but she doesn't turn me on; only you do, baby!" Mike kissed Bips passionately.

CHAPTER 17

THE GANG IS BACK

On Friday night Angela got a call.

"Hey, baby doll."

"Hey what's up, cool dude?"

"I hardly could get your number. Why you changed it?"

"Long story, Mike."

"Angela, we need your help . . . Bips and me."

"Alright, guys, I am sure you know where to find me."

Later in the evening she got call from security "Madam, you have guests." Angela opened the door with biometric fingerprint scanner. Two strangers were sitting in her hall.

"Excuse me, who are you?" Angela asked.

"Angela, it's me."

"Oh, my God! Mike, what happened to your face?"

Bipasha and Mike told her the whole story. "That's incredible, guys," Angela said.

"Angela, so can you talk to Alex? Is he on our side?"

"Well, actually I don't talk to him. We broke off."

"You did what?" Bips and Mike could not believe it.

"Yes, we broke off . . . but, guys, let's talk about something else."

"OK, Angela, sorry," Mike said.

"Angela, but what do we do now? We need Alex. We can't hack the system without him," Bipasha asked.

"I am sorry, guys, but I can't help you with that."

Angelas's phone rang:

"Hey, kitten, how are you?" Vlad called.

"I am fine, Vlad."

"Let's go out, tonight, baby."

"OK, cool."

"My driver will pick you up at 11.30, baby."

"I am inviting two friends . . ."

"No problem, kitten," the oligarch interrupted, "You can invite the whole city. See you soon, baby!"

"Bye, Vlad."

"Bipasha, Mike, you have to be ready in an hour."

Bipasha and Mike were impressed by the place. They never partied at such a fancy club before: girls in tight designer dresses, holding Prada, LV and Gucci purses; guys in Tom Ford and Zegna suits. The smell of cigars mixed with French perfume and liquor surrounded them. It was the world of ultra luxury. Finally, Bipasha and Mike noticed Vlad. The oligarch was very handsome. He reminded lion: dangerous, powerful and magnificent.

"So what do you think about Vlad, Bipasha?" Angela asked.

"He is just perfect . . . but Angela, he is not Alex." Angela felt sad and empty.

"Excuse me, get us new bottle of Dom Perignon," Angela ordered. The waiter nodded.

"Sweetheart, if you drink so much champagne I will have to carry you home," Vlad joked. Angela smiled.

Alex entered the club. He felt unwelcome. People who used to smile and chat with him before, now avoided him. Anyway, Alex had no choice: he had to give money back to Angela. He is not a thief.

He saw Vlad. Oligarch was in very happy mood laughing and chatting . . . with Angela. Angela noticed Alex. She was stunning. Alex looked at Angela and he knew again that she was *The One* . . . Well, now the one who was is in oligarch's arms. Alex felt sharp pain. The legs felt so heavy. He hardly could move.

"Wow! Alex superstar is back, I guess I need to call Masha and Dasha to give you massage so you won't feel bored," supermodel Natasha said. Everybody laughed. It felt like everyone read that stupid newspaper.

Vlad stared at Alex; he looked like a lion ready to take the jump.

"This b..tard . . . what does he want?" Vlad thought.

Angela looked at Alex. There was so much pain in her beautiful eyes.

"Angela, I have to give you this . . ."

"What is that?" Angela asked.

"Your cheque, your money. I was . . . I was out of country. So . . . anyway, I am sorry. I need to go now." Alex left.

Everybody looked at Vlad.

"Well, everyone, cheers for Angela's new cheque . . . Let's party, guys!"

* * *

Alex could not sleep. Angela is with Vlad. Why? Does she love him? Are they serious?

* * *

Angela woke up with horrible headache; she drank too much last night. She went to kitchen.

"Angela, I will make a cup of coffee for you, it will make you feel better," as if reading her thoughts Bipasha said.

"Here is your coffee."

"Tastes great, thanks, Bips."

"Angela, you need to talk to Alex," Bipasha asked again.

"I am sorry, Bips. I can't."

"OK, leave it, Bips. I will talk to him," Mike said.

"But, guys, it is very risky. What if he doesn't want to take the school down?"

"I need to take the risk, Angela."

Alex got message. "Who could break his tablet security? Must be Mike," Alex thought.

"Hi, Alex, it's me, your friend."

"Hey, how are you?"

"Alex, can you meet me at coffee shop near Nevskiy prospect, 50?" Mike typed.

"Dude, I am too famous for that. Let's meet at my suite. Come to my hotel," Alex answered.

"Be careful guys it can be trap . . . Guys, take my car and driver," Angela said.

"Thanks, Angela."

*   *   *

Bipasha and Mike entered the suite. Alex told security to let them in.

"Sorry, who are you?" Alex asked.

"I am Mike, Alex."

"Oh, what happened, Mike?"

Mike told him everything.

"So, Alex, are you going to help us?"

Alex smiled, "You know, Mike, Cheng and Aimee—all of us are trying to break the school's code."

Mike and Bips felt relieved. Alex called Aimee and Cheng. Cheng, Aimee, Bipasha, Alex and Mike chatted, cracked jokes, laughed. They felt really happy and safe together. After long time the gang was back. Finally, Cheng had the courage to say what everybody felt, "Guys, we need Angela. We can't do it without Angela. We need to talk to her." Everybody looked at Alex.

"OK, guys, I will call her," Alex promised.

The phone rang. Angela saw the number. It was Alex. She could not believe it. So many times she was dreaming that he would call. She was imagining for hours how he would talk to her and what she would answer him. And then after some time she lost hope. Now, it was for real, but she didn't know what to do. Should she answer it at all? After some thought, she pressed answer.

"Hi, Angela. It is Alex. I am really sorry about what I told you. I know that you are happy with Vlad and I have no right to ask you to risk your life. But if one day you change your mind please join our team."

Angela answered after long pause, "Alex . . . I will think about it." She disconnected. She couldn't stop crying. "Happy with Vlad? Why does Alex want to hurt her more? He left her. How can he talk to her like that now?" Angela thought.

CHAPTER 18

SANDRA

"Sandra," Professor Goldman called, "Come here sweetheart." She was so pretty and fresh. Sandra was just 21 years old. Professor took her to the room. "I want you to remove your clothes."

She felt disgusted, "Please don't touch me, professor!"

"Come on, sweetheart, just show me your breasts." Sandra tried to fight back, but felt weak; she realized Professor Goldman mixed drugs in her drink. He opened her blouse and grabbed her.

"You are so fresh, so young," Professor Goldman whispered. Sandra could hardly move; her body was paralyzed in a way she never felt before. Sandra could not believe what was happening with her. Professor Goldman whom she respected so much turned into this sick evil creature. "If only I could fight back . . . I would have killed this monster!" Sandra thought, feeling helpless.

Finally, Professor Goldman finished his disgusting act. "Tomorrow, Sandra, I expect more from you." She felt horrified. "Be ready, Sandra, I will be back," Professor Goldman left the room. Sandra was lying in complete darkness. She was scared. She didn't understand why professor became evil. He used to say she was like his daughter.

In the morning Professor Goldman came back. He held a gun in his hand. Sandra felt terrified. "Come with me," professor ordered. Sandra had no doubt that these were the last moments of her life. Professor and Sandra went through long corridors. "Stand in the corner there," he ordered. Professor put his id card on scanner to enter the lab. "Come in, Sandra!" She entered the lab. It was horrible. There were hundreds of students. Sandra recognized some of her friends.

Here she was: her best friend–Lisa; she had such beautiful violet eyes. Sandra ran towards her friend. Lisa opened her eyes, Sandra screamed. Lisa's beautiful eyes were missing. She whispered, "Sandra, is that you? Professor Goldman did this to me. He cut my eyes out."

Professor Goldman took Sandra back to the room.

"Why are you doing this to me? Professors will arrest you! You will go to prison for the rest of your life!" Sandra shouted.

"Oh, really, Sandra? Who will arrest me? All of the professors decided that are you are useless. Sweetheart, your intelligence level is very low, the school does not need you anymore. The only thing that keeps you alive is that I like you. I will come back tomorrow night. You have to be ready. You have to make your professor very happy, my sweetheart. Remember, there are many other pretty students who can make professor happy. You are lucky: I chose you." Professor locked the room and left the her alone. Sandra did not know what to do. She did not want to sleep with sleazy Professor Goldman . . . but she didn't want to die. Sandra knew the professor could do anything to her. World seemed to be such a cruel place. Nobody was there to save her.

CHAPTER 19

DANCE OF DEATH

Fedya was lying on the floor in pool of blood . . . his blo3od. The gangsters just left. Next time they will kill him. These people have no mercy: for them it is pure business. He has no chance. The bottle of vodka was lying on the floor next to him. He took a sip directly from bottle. Fedya felt a relief. The pain seemed to be subsiding. He remembered his previous life.

"Fedor, the young star of Russian ballet," the press praised him, "Fedor's seemingly gravity-defying leaps are as perfect as those of the greatest Vaslav Nijinsky; and Fedor's dynamic pirouettes remind us of the legendary Rudolf Nureyev."

Fedya remembered his mother, simple woman, who worked long shifts, cleaning toilets day and night to pay out his tuition bills . . . and now she looked so happy in an elegant Versace dress, sitting at the first row with all rich and famous people. Fedya recollected his mother's smile when the audience gave him a standing ovation . . . and how his mother shouted proudly, "That's my son!"

He was the lead ballet dancer at the famous Mariinksy theatre. The same Mariinksy theatre that was once called Imperial—and where for 300 years the legends of Russian ballet performed in front of tsars and nobility.

The world was at Fedor's feet . . . and then his thoughts went to Borya, the gay guy, who had neither style nor technique of Fedya. Fedor remembered Borya, whispering to his ear, "You will fall Fedya! You are too straight. Ballet is not for straight guys, Fedya! . . . even Nijinsky had to get support from Diaghilev!"

Fedor ignored Borya completely. After getting a loan, Fedya and his mother moved into a new big apartment. Life seemed to be perfect! Then one rainy evening he was driving home in his BMW, suddenly some car hit from behind, he lost control of his vehicle. Fedya could hardly remember the accident. He woke up in a hospital room. First thing Fedya noticed was his left leg; he had a plaster on it. Fedya was so scared. Will he ever dance again?

Borya entered the room and smiled like a snake, "I brought you flowers, Fedya . . . who knows maybe your last ones. Did the doctors tell you, Fedya? I guess they didn't. I don't think you will ever dance again. By the way, I am replacing you in the ballet. You were too young for this success, you didn't deserve it. Fedya, you don't understand ballet is not about art, but about whom you spend time with and how you make the important people happy."

"Just get lost. Go away, Borya !" Fedya shouted.

After the plaster was removed, Fedya's leg was not the same. The doctor told him, it would take at least 6-10 months to get back in shape. To pay out a loan for the apartment Fedya became a dance instructor in city's most popular clubs: Gala Dance, Casa Latina, Divadance. He learnt most exotic forms of dancing–whatever students were ready to pay for–from Egyptian *Saidi* to Cuban *Cha-cha-cha*. It seemed liked there was no single rhythm that Fedor was not familiar with. It was great fun to learn, but money was not easy. All those sleazy ladies, dancing closer than necessary, trying to rub his body, giving him hints that they want individual lessons at their homes . . . It was just horrible! Fedor missed Mariinksy: his troupe, his stage. He could tolerate all this shit only to pay out loan for the apartment. Six months have passed: Fedor's leg was almost perfect. A few more weeks and he will try to get back for auditions at Mariinksy and if they don't give him soloist role, he can go to Mikhailovksy theatre. He will not give up!

Then came the worst day of his life! His mother . . . Fedya had one more sip of vodka. The surgery had to be done next week! He had no money. He needed 200 K euro! He sold anything he could, but it was not enough. Then, Fedya met a friend, who told him to try Forex, within the first week of trading different currencies, he lost all his money.

Somebody is knocking at the door. "Must be the gangsters. What do they want now?" he thought.

"Come in, join the party," Fedor shouted.

No . . . not gangsters! Maybe he was just too drunk or was it Alex the superstar for real? In this dark room Alex looked like Greek God. "How can anybody be so handsome?" Fedor thought. Alex's beauty gave creepy feeling in real life. When Fedor first saw Alex on TV he was sure it was just all about good lights and digital effects . . . but here in this room Alex looked just too perfect to be human.

"Hi, Fedya, my name is Alex."

"Yes, Superstar Alex," Fedya said, "I saw you on TV."

"Great."

Fedya tried to stand up, but he couldn't.

"I heard you need money."

"Yes, it is true," Fedya confirmed. He was surprised that Alex behaved in such a normal way: Alex had no starry airs. "But unless you pay 200 K euro for my mother's surgery and 50 K euro to gangsters, I am not interested."

"OK, Fedya, done. In fact, I will pay out your apartment loan as well."

"Alex, I didn't know they pay so much in your troupe. I may need to forget Mariinksy."

"Well, the thing is, Fedya, you may die if you don't dance correctly . . . are you still interested?"

"The gangsters will kill me any way, Alex."

"Alright, then I need to take your audition."

"Now . . . I am slightly out shape, Alex." Fedya tried to stand up again, but fell down.

"No problem, Fedya, just listen to this: *dum tak tak dum tak.*"

"It is *Maqsoum*, Alex, Egyptian rhythm."

"OK," Alex seemed slightly puzzled.

"Well, Fedya, do I get it right? There are two notes: '*dum*' is heavy note played in the center of the drum and '*tak*' is light one played on the edge of drum. So, the rhytm is it 1 2 2 1 2, correct?"

"Yes, I mean you can say it that way, Alex."

"OK, Fedya, what about this one: *Ta di mi / Ta ka di mi //*?

"Alex, that is Indian *Tala* to be exact *Chaurastra Eka Tala.*"

"OK, Fedya, how many beats does it have?"

"4, Alex."

"Cool, Fedya, what about this one?"

"Come on, Alex, you must be joking, right? You are trying to test me, Russian classical dancer, and you make me listen to Tchaikovsky. That's just funny."

"So, Fedya, you know most of world rhythms, right?"

"Well, I guess so, Alex, I worked in all these dance clubs . . ."

"Congratulations, Fedya, you are hired!"

"But I don't understand, Alex . . . You did not even check my dance?"

"Don't worry, Fedya. I will explain all; but not now. We can't waste any more time."

Alex called his assistants. "Guys, help Fedya to take a shower and get dressed. Fedya, don't forget your passport, you will need it."

Fedya felt better in the limousine of Alex. Surprisingly, Angela was sitting there as well.

"Hi, Fedya, I am a great fan of yours," Angela said.

"Thanks, Angela. You look great in your ads," Fedya answered. "Strange," Fedya thought, "Why is Angela with Alex . . . didn't they break off? Angela was dating now Vlad–the oligarch."

"Where are we going now, Alex?" Fedya asked.

"First to hospital, Fedya, then to the plane," Alex answered.

*   *   *

The doctor informed him, "Fedor, money for your mother's surgery was already transferred. Your mother will be fine!" Fedya almost felt like crying. Ward no 23: he entered the room, his mother looked very pale.

"Fedenka my son, how are you?" she asked.

"I am fine, Mom. Don't worry, Mom. All will be OK. You have the best doctors around you. Sorry, I need to leave now, Mom," Fedya said and went towards the exit. Fedya turned back and looked at his mother again. Maybe it would be the last time he would ever see her. Death could come soon to take him away.

Alex's limo reached the private plane parking. The documents check was went smoothly. In the jet Alex gave him a blindfold: "Sorry, Fedya, you need to wear this." The plane took off. Fedya felt very tired and fell asleep immediately.

Fedya woke up when the jet landed. The limo was already ready for them. Fedya still had to wear a blindfold; and then he was taken into some building.

"Fedya, you can remove the blindfold now," Alex said. Fedya was at canteen. All kinds of food were served there.

"Have your food, Fedya, and we will discuss your assignment."

"Guys, I present you Fedya . . ." Alex said.

"I know him," Bips said, "you are the sensation of Mariinksy."

"Was," Fedya interrupted.

"Don't worry, Fedya," Cheng said, "if you survive next Monday we will help you to get your ballet roles back!"

"But Borya . . . replaced me."

"He may slip and break his leg," smiled Cheng, "just like you got into accident."

"You mean, Borya did that to me?"

Alex reminded, "Guys, leave all this and let's concentrate on our problem. Fedya, you go and take some rest. Tomorrow we will start."

"Bye, Fedya."

"Bye, guys."

"Mike, what about the code?"

"Well, Alex, it could be better. We only managed to crack 30 percent . . . we got some weird girl's name—Ana Crus," Mike replied.

"That's strange, Mike . . ." Alex was deep in his thoughts.

"Alex, can you explain to me what you are trying to do? Why did you bring Fedya?" Bipasha asked.

"OK, guys, I will explain. But first, let's convert whatever code we cracked into music rhythm."

"Alex, it's crazy. How can we do it?" Cheng protested.

"Relax, Cheng, it is not hard. Just catch the pattern:

Fibonacci code word 11 i.e. implied distribution 1/4

Next Fibonacci code word 011 has implied distribution 1/8, then 0011 into 1/16, Cheng, can you see the pattern? These are beats: 1/4 = crotchet; 1/8 is quaver and 1/16 equals to semiquaver," Alex explained.

"Oh," Bips interrupted, "so that's why you brought Fedya."

"Exactly, Bips! Fedya knows most of the time signatures as he is a fabulous dancer."

*   *   *

Fedya woke up. He felt happy for the first time in a long while. Even if he dies . . . his mother will be saved!

"Hi, Alex," Fedya said.

"Hi, Fedya," Alex answered.

"OK, Fedya, are you ready? You had your food?"

"Yes, Alex, thanks I am ready," Fedya said.

"Mike, are you ready?" Alex asked.

"Yes, Alex."

"Fedya, what do you hear now?"

"It is *masmoudi*, this rhytm belongs to Berber tribe–of North Africa."

"OK, Fedya, great. Is it 6/8?"

"No, Alex, it is 4/8."

"Mike, is it working?" Alex asked.

"It does. But, guys, I have very bad news. We got caught."

"Shit! How long do we have?"

"3 minutes, Alex."

"Guys, we won't be able to make it on time if we run now," Cheng interrupted.

"Let's not panic!" Alex said in a calm voice, "We have no option, but to crack the code. Let's do it!"

Fedya looked totally scared.

"Fedya, relax you can do it. You have to do it. Concentrate, man!" Cheng said.

"Angela, Cheng, Bips try to win us more time. Mike, let's go ahead," Alex shouted.

Alex converted next file, "What is it, Fedya?"

"That's Turkish *Karsilama*: 9/8 rhytm, Alex."

"Guys, hurry up we only have 6 minutes and 40 seconds left," Mike warned.

"OK, Fedya, next rhytm!" Alex said.

"Well, Alex, that's weird . . . OK! I got it "t*empo di valse*" it is waltz, guys, ¾."

Fedya kept recognizing the rhytms. He was brilliant.

Mike shouted, "Fedya, it actually stopped working, something is wrong. Guys, we got only 5 minutes before they send the bomb".

"That's not possible I can't be wrong I am familiar with all those rhythms," Fedya protested.

"Of course, guys–Ana Crus," Alex shouted.

"Alex! Oh, God, he is losing it," Bipasha cried.

"It is not Ana Crus–the name of a female. It is the Greek term–*anacrusis*," Alex continued, "Fedya, you tell them."

"Well, it is basically a note or a few notes that precede the first downbeat in the bar," Fedya explained.

"Guys, cut the music theory part . . . If we can't break the code we will all die!" shouted Mike.

"I don't know guys! I am also confused," Fedya admitted.

"Fedya, you forgot the main part," Alex said, "In Western tradition the composers are normally advised to delete . . ."

"Yes, of course, Alex, to delete corresponding number of beats from the final bar so that it would match the whole peace," Fedya interrupted.

"Exactly, Fedya, so we need to start deleting the last digits, guys."

"Mike, what you got?" Alex asked.

"12456468214 . . . Alex!"

"Delete last six digits," Alex said.

"40 seconds," Bips counted, "20 seconds!" These could be last seconds of their lives: "10, 9, 8, 7 . . ."

"Guys, it worked! We broke the code!" shouted Mike.

Angela, Bipasha, Alex, Mike, Cheng, Aimee, Fedya–everybody felt so happy! They were never 100 per cent sure if they could make it. The feeling was incredible; they just got a second chance at life!

After first minutes of joy Bipasha said, "Guys, we still can't make it on our own. We just managed to break their code, they can't bomb us, but we still can't attack the school. There are too many of them."

"You are right but don't worry about that, Bips. I have a plan," Mike smiled.

*   *   *

The police officer picked up the phone. "Yes . . . What? . . . Don't be scared, child! Where are you? . . . You can't see anything . . . They do what? Don't worry, child, we will rescue you!"

The TV channel got call: "Hi, I just managed to get hot stuff . . . You like it? That's what I thought. What is location? . . . Alright, I will give you all information. But, listen, I am trying to get break as a reporter so I want my name to be mentioned . . . OK, then it's a deal. Write down the location."

A few other channels got similar calls from mysterious wannabe reporter.

In an hour time the castle was surrounded by TV reporters, journalists, police officers and ambulance staff.

"The mountain is quite high. We will need helicopter to attack the castle," said the captain.

"Sir, we have to be extra careful. The wind is too strong. The landing can be dangerous," warned lieutenant.

Alex, Mike, Angela, Aimee, Cheng and Bipasha arrived in black limo.

"Who gave you permission?" the captain shouted.

"We are with AGS Secret Service, Sir, we are here to assist you as it is matter of national security."

"Never heard of such a secret service."

"That's why it is called secret service, Sir."

"Can I see your IDs?"

"Please, Sir," Alex said.

"I don't know. Sounds suspicious," the captain mumbledchecking their documents, "OK, anyway . . . How you can help us?"

"As per our information there is a secret passage between the rocks. If you give us enough people we can enter the castle from there."

"Oh, OK. Seems like we have no choice. The wind is too strong for a helicopter to land near the castle. Let's try your passage," captain agreed.

"Mike, make sure security alarm is off," Alex said.

"Cheng and Aimee, you will go to lab. Bipasha, Angela and me—we will go to the professor's room."

They entered the building: Alex had mixed feelings, he used to call this place home. Now he came here to destroy his home. "The professor's room is there: first door on the left. Kill anyone who tries to stop you; otherwise you will get killed. Do not remove your gas masks," Alex ordered. The policemen nodded.

Alex threw a gas grenade on the floor and broke the door, the professors looked shocked. They could not believe anybody could attack them. The professors always believed the castle's security system was the best in the world. Nobody would be able to hack it. The policemen handcuffed the professors, read them their rights and arrested them.

Cheng shouted, "Follow me! Break the door of this room. Shoot anyone, who tries to attack you. These people are dangerous and armed." Policemen broke the door. Sandra, beautiful young woman begged, "Please don't rape me!"

"Sandra, it's me Cheng."

"Cheng? Why are you wearing gas mask?"

"Cause we throw gas grenades. Come with us, Sandra. We will not hurt you." Sandra started crying. "Don't cry, Sandra, it's all over. You are safe now. Sandra, you know where they keep other students?" Cheng asked. Sandra nodded.

*　　*　　*

In the evening it was all over. Hundreds of students were rescued. Some of the kids were already reunited with families. The students looked happy, most of them were crying, but those were tears of happiness. Professors said they were victims and were forced to teach at the castle against their will. But professors could not get away with lies anymore. Students from the lab room told media how professors removed children's organs, raped them and enjoyed it. TV channels kept showing 21 year old Sandra, shouting: "You wanted to rape me tonight, Professor Goldman!"

The Professor smiled at cameras and said, "Sandra, you are like my daughter. I would never touch you. Why are you lying, my child?"

"Professor, I am ready to take any lie detector test!" The fear could be clearly read in the professor's eyes.

"I need a lawyer," Professor Goldman mumbled.

The camera zoomed into a police woman face, she was disgusted. The woman put her arm around Sandra's shoulders and pulled her away. It was clear: Professor Goldman would be going to jail for a long time.

CHAPTER 20

VICTORY IS OURS

"We won," Angela said.

"It would not be possible without Fedya, that guy did great job," Aimee interrupted, "What happened to him?"

"He is back at Mariinksy. Fedya is soloist again. Borya got a very interesting offer at Bolshoy, and he is now in Moscow," Alex answered.

"You paid for Borya's contract at Bolshoy?" Bips asked.

"Yes, Bips, it was the least I could do for him."

"Great decision," Cheng admired.

"Well, guys, I am just so happy we won," Angela said.

"Yes, Angela, we won the battle, but not the war. I think they will start new school somewhere else: some remote country. They will kidnap bright, good looking kids," Alex said.

"If the parents of missing children keep searching for the kids, they will kill the parents also," Cheng interrupted, "I saw the files, guys. Our parents were killed by them. They didn't die at accident like the professors told us."

"I know, Cheng, we also hacked the files," Angela answered after long pause, "I just hope the professors who were involved in these dirty things, will spend the rest of their lives in jail."

"Angela, the worst thing is that the bosses will do the same thing with new children. They will start selection process and then turn the best chosen kids into murderers. It is just a question of time," Alex continued.

"I agree, Alex, unfortunately, guys, the agent's school is perfect business model. Elite professional killer will charge at least 100 K euro per each contract. That's what they roughly spend to raise one kid here at the castle. Practically, after the first contract, they pay out their investment. Then it is just pure profit for them," Cheng said.

"Don't forget, Cheng, they get extra income from the sale of children's organs," Bipasha added.

"The scary thing is that it could happen to anyone. Any family is not safe. They can kidnap kids from kindergarten, school. Any kid with great intelligence is at risk. And if parents investigate too much . . . they just kill them," Angela said.

"So what you want to do, Alex?" Mike asked.

"We must catch the big fish who funds all these operations. I am afraid the truth is very ugly," Alex answered.

"I agree with you, Alex" Cheng interrupted, "after the murder of the minister stock markets responded immediately. Somebody made huge money."

"So do you think hedge funds involved?" Alex said.

"Could be," Cheng answered.

"Politicians?" Bipasha asked.

"Most probably," Angela suggested.

"And the level?" Aimee asked.

"International at least . . . but I suspect it's global," Alex replied.

*   *   *

The Hollywood director told producer:

"Hey, Matt, it is on each and every channel! Are you watching? They kidnapped small kids! They raped girls! It is disgusting! How can anybody be so sick? They wanted to raise elite professional killers . . . the thing is that it could happen to anybody's bright child. It could be your family or my family. Nobody is safe. Matt, you know what I smell? I smell big money in this story."

"Do you, Sanny?"

"Yes, absolutely. It is something that any family with bright kid could relate to. You know, Matt, we need to cast a fresh face. We will get a good publicity just by saying: based on true events blah blah . . . I am telling you it is better subject than Facebook or Apple . . . or that Slumdog millionaire."

*   *   *

Alex's phone rang a few days later.

"Is it, Alex?"

"Hi, Alex, My name is Sanny Pincher. I got the number from your manager. I liked your work in that video. I wanted to know if you are interested to act."

"Well, honestly, Mr. Pincher, I never thought about it . . . but yes I would love to!"

"Also, Alex, I wanted to ask you that girl An . . . Angela, right? Can she act? You seem to have good chemistry so bring her also . . ."

"OK, Sir, so when you want to meet us ?"

"I don't have much time, Alex! Next Thursday is OK for you? If you have US visa issue we can meet in Europe."

"No I don't have any problem, Sir."

"OK, Alex, so see you."

Alex thought again and again . . . Should he call her? What if she says no? Anyway, he can at least try!

"Hi, Angela."

"Hi, Alex."

"I got offer from Hollywood producer he is interested to meet us next Thursday."

"Who? . . . Wow! He is big director! I am coming, Alex."

Alex felt so happy! Vlad is the oligarch, but he is Angela's first love. Alex hoped Angela still loves him.

*　　*　　*

Finally, on Thursday morning they met at Hollywood producer's office.

"So happy you could make it, guys. See, I hope it is between us–I plan my movie on that agent's school–you know all that stuff on news channels. I want people to know more about it."

"Sir, believe me it is great story," Alex agreed.

"OK, Alex, my main action guy is here why don't you go with him? Change into something comfortable . . . and show me what I can expect."

*   *   *

"OK, the scene is like that: you guys are fighting in the room, then you need to run together through the broken door, sit on the bike and Alex will drive the bike till the final mark," the action guy showed. "Here is your first mark and that one is your final mark. It doesn't matter if you didn't learn martial arts; just make the fight scene look believable!"

"Camera!" the action director ordered.

"Rolling, Sir!" his first assistant answered.

"Action!" the director shouted.

Alex had to fight a big African man. The guy was a total pro. He hit Alex just hard enough to look real on camera. Alex also controlled his force.

Angela's opponent was a Thai girl. She was bitchy. The Thai girl almost tried to scratch Angela's nose and then kicked with full force in Angela's stomach. Angela decided: enough to be sweet with the girl! Next time the babe tried to scratch her cheek; she twisted Thai girl's hand and threw her on the floor with full force.

"OK, Angela, Alex, now run towards the bike. Alex, start the bike," first assistant said.

"Cut," the action director shouted.

"How are they?" the movie director asked the action master.

"Fantastic, man, they had a stunt background?"

"No, Alex, he is Russian star singer and Angela is top model."

"Sanny, I am surprised they don't have any stunt experience, I haven't seen anything like that. It almost feels they are highly trained stuntmen or Special Forces."

Sanny was happy, he shouted, "Angela, Alex, please change and come to my office."

A few minutes later Angela and Alex came to the producer's office.

"Coffee?" the office assistant offered.

"No, thanks."

"Guys, you did stunts really well . . . but can you do some cold reading for me," the director asked.

"Yes, sure," Alex answered.

"OK, Alex and Angela that's your script, scene 21," director gave them two pages.

"Let me know once you are ready, guys," the director said.

Ten minutes later Alex looked at Angela, "Are you ready?" he asked.

"Yes, Alex."

They asked an assistant to call the director.

"OK, guys, so can you read the scene for me? Where is your script, anyway?"

"That's OK, Sir, we know the lines."

"No, I need exact lines!" The assistant brought the script.

"So how is it going, bro, did you manage to hack the system?" Alex asked. Mr. Pincher kept reading the script, while Angela and Alex said their lines. Their voices seemed to be fine: full of expressions, with perfect modulation. Director looked up and realized they did not read, but knew their lines by heart: word to word. He was shocked, "but, guys, when did you manage to learn this stuff by heart?"

"We had around ten minutes, Sir".

"Wow! How is it possible: some new system?"

"That's our secret," Alex smiled, "If we tell you, we will have to kill you!"

The director grinned. He was super excited: "Alex and Angela had full package: looks, talent, and sex appeal." Who knows after so many nominations, this time with Alex and Angela in his movie, he may finally get an Oscar for the best director. Sanny almost imagined accepting the award: it was an amazing feeling.

"OK, guys, you did great job . . . Well, of course I need to work on you. But I believe in you, guys."

"Thank you, Sir."

"How are they?" the producer asked the director after Angela and Alex left.

"Phenomenal, Matt! We need to sign Alex and Angela before somebody else steals them. They are star material."

* * *

"So, Alex, it seems like a great ending—we are getting the Hollywood movie."

"I have a feeling, it is only the beginning, Angela. But with this money and fame we can finally start the war and save many kids from hell that we lived in!"

"Alex, so you want to be the hero who saves the world and protects innocent children?" Angela laughed.

"Why not, Angela?"

"Well, I guess . . . You have it in you, Alex!"

"Thanks . . . Listen, Angela, we did really well today at audition. Can I . . . can you . . . you want to meet for a coffee . . . or drink tonight?"

"I will think about it, Alex."

"So is it yes?"

"I already said, I will think about it, Alex."

"But there is a chance, right?"

"Don't push your luck too much, Alex."

"Hope never dies, Angela. I will wait for your call."